DEAD
SILENCE

>a MIKE & RIEL MYSTERY >>>

DEAD
SILENCE

NORAH MCCLINTOCK

darbycreek

MINNEAPOLIS

Darby Creek
A division of Lerner Publishing Group, Inc.
241 First Avenue North
Minneapolis, MN 55401 USA

For reading levels and more information, look up this title at
www.lernerbooks.com.

Front Cover: © iStockphoto.com/Peeterv.

Main body text set in Janson Text LT Std 11.5/15.
Typeface provided by Adobe Systems.

Library of Congress Cataloging-in-Publication Data

McClintock, Norah.
        Dead silence / by Norah McClintock.
            pages   cm. — (Mike & Riel ; #5)
        Originally published by Scholastic Canada, 2008.
        Summary: Mike's friend has been murdered, and he is determined to
find out who did it.
        ISBN 978–1–4677–2609–2 (lib. bdg. : alk. paper)
        ISBN 978–1–4677–2620–7 (eBook)
        [1. Mystery and detective stories. 2. Murder—Fiction. 3. Foster home
care—Fiction.] I. Title.
PZ7.M478414184De 2014
[Fic]—dc23   2013017570

Manufactured in the United States of America
1 – SB – 12/31/13

GARY PUBLIC LIBRARY

CHAPTER ONE

You can't always tell when your whole life is going to change, not even when it's just about to happen. You don't always see it coming. I didn't. It was the second week of October, which meant that every day seemed pretty much like every other day: get up, go to school, do your homework, put in some hours at a part-time job, and, if you're lucky, have a little fun. Mostly it's boring, but that's the worst you can say about it. You start to think that things are always going to be the way they are right now. You wonder if anything is ever going to change. You wish it would. I sure did. But you know what? If I'd known what was in store, I would have wished for everything to stay exactly the way it was.

The day before everything changed, I got up at the regular time. I went downstairs and had my regular breakfast—100 percent organic cereal washed down with a big glass of organic orange juice. I was on my own that morning. Riel and Susan had both left early for work. I got my stuff together, looked at the clock, and realized that if I hurried, I could swing by Rebecca's place and we could walk to school together. So that's exactly what I did.

We got to school a couple of minutes before the bell rang. The morning dragged by: homeroom, math, history, and, finally, lunch. Rebecca had band practice, and I had plans to hook up with Sal. We were going to walk to the food court at Gerrard Square, a mall near school.

I went to meet Sal at his locker. He was skimming through his *Driver's Handbook*. He wanted me to quiz him while we ate because he was going downtown the next day at lunchtime to take his written test for his driver's license. You'd think he was taking an exam to be a brain surgeon or something, the way he was going at it.

"You must have that whole thing memorized by now," I said.

He shrugged and handed me his biology binder. I opened it to take out the pages I needed to copy.

"Take the whole binder," Sal said.

"But I only need the notes from yesterday." I'd missed class because of a dentist appointment.

"I've got everything organized, Mike. Just take the whole binder and make sure you give it back to me in class tomorrow, okay?"

"Okay," I said, even though the binder was bulky. He had a lot of stuff in there so early in the year. Sal had turned into a super-organized guy. He liked things just so, and since he was doing me a favor, I figured I should go along with him.

He closed his locker.

"Can you come with me tomorrow when I do the test, Mike?" he said.

"Me? What for?"

"Moral support." Sal is pretty smart, but taking tests makes him nervous.

"Sure," I said. "That's what friends are for, right?"

He looked at me like he had something on his mind, something he wanted to tell me or ask me. But he didn't say anything. He just nodded. We made our way downstairs.

On the way, I told him he was lucky that he was going to learn to drive. I wished I could, too, but what car would I drive? If I had parents, like Sal did, that would be one thing. His parents had an old beater that they didn't drive much, especially now that his dad was sick and his mom had a new full-time job that she could get to on the subway. It was different for me. If I wanted to learn to drive, I'd have to ask Riel if I could use his car, and I couldn't picture myself doing that. I was afraid he would say he didn't think I was responsible enough for that.

When I said that to Sal, he laughed. Then, just like that, the laugh died and Sal's face turned white. I'm not kidding. It was like someone had thrown a bucket of white paint at him. I looked where he was looking, which was out at the street.

It was the same scene as every other day at lunchtime, especially in nice weather like it was that day. There were kids everywhere, standing on the sidewalk, walking around, jaywalking to get to the other side of the street where their friends were or to get to some store or restaurant. I saw all the same people I saw every day—a bunch of girls up near the corner, including a couple of Rebecca's friends, Kim and Luci. I saw the new kid, Alex, a guy a lot of people made fun of—which, if you ask me, was mean. He'd been in some kind of accident when he was younger. It wasn't his fault he was the way he was. High school is bad enough. But being different in high school? You might as well walk around with a target painted on your back because, no matter what you do, there are always some kids who are going to take shots at you. They sure did at Alex. He was out there all alone, staring at a bunch of kids across the street, looking like he wished he could be part of everything instead of separate. And directly opposite the school, making a lot of noise just like always, were the kids Alex was looking at—Teddy Carlin and Bailey Zackery and the rest of them.

Oh.

I glanced at Sal.

"Don't worry," I said. "If Teddy tries to give you a hard time again, he'll have to deal with me, too."

The color came back into Sal's face. He shook his head and laughed, like he was embarrassed that I'd caught him looking so scared. When he turned to me, he had the same look on his face that I had seen when I was at his locker.

"There's something I have to tell you, Mike," he said. "It's something I probably should have told you a while ago."

But before he could say what it was, Rebecca came

through the door and hooked one of her arms through mine. "Mr. Korchak had some kind of special meeting he had to go to. Practice is postponed until tomorrow," she said. Mr. Korchak was the music teacher at my school. "Where are you and Sal going? Can I come?"

I glanced at Sal. He smiled at Rebecca. He really liked her. Sometimes he teased me and said he couldn't figure out what a girl like her was doing with a guy like me. I was sure he wouldn't mind if she tagged along. But he said, "I have to study for my driver's test. You guys go ahead."

"I thought you wanted me to quiz you," I said.

"I'll help," Rebecca said.

But Sal shook his head. "It's okay. I have to concentrate. But thanks anyway."

He started down the steps.

"Wait," I said. "You were going to tell me something."

"It can wait."

"I'll meet you after school. You can tell me then."

"I can't," he said. "I'm tutoring, then I have work."

That night, when I opened Sal's binder to copy his biology notes, I saw a pink envelope tucked into the back pocket. It had big loopy handwriting on it. I guess that should have told me something. I was staring at it when the phone rang. It was Sal, calling me on his break. Looking back, I wish he hadn't. Maybe then things wouldn't have turned out the way they did.

» » »

5

The very next day, everything changed. And I mean everything.

Here's the way it happened:

I walked to school alone that day. I couldn't have gone with Rebecca even if I'd wanted to. She had to be at school early to meet with the rest of her team for some special lab project she was doing in biology. She said she would meet me at my locker before the bell rang. I hurried to school. I got there a little earlier than usual, which is exactly what I had planned. But Rebecca's team meeting must have finished early, too, because she almost gave me a heart attack when she showed up a lot sooner than I expected, before I was ready for her. I slammed my locker door and spun around to face her. She was smiling at me, the way she almost always does. But I knew she wouldn't be smiling much longer. I took a deep breath. Then I broke the news to her and braced myself for her reaction. Besides being my girlfriend, Rebecca is the nicest person I know. But she's also one of those people who is always on time, is always prepared, and never forgets anything. So I was pretty sure she would freak out when I told her that I had forgotten her history textbook at home. Sure enough, she did.

"I *need* that book, Mike, and you *promised* me you wouldn't lose it," she said, loud enough that Teddy Carlin, whose locker was directly across the hall from mine, turned to look. So did all his friends, who were always hanging around Teddy. Teddy smirked at me like I had to be the biggest loser in the world to have a girl giving me grief right there in the middle of the hall. Teddy was one of those guys who like to be the center of attention, and he was having an easy time of it this year, now that A. J. Siropolous and his gang were out of the school. Some of them were even locked up. "And you can't even lend me your book," Rebecca said, "because you can't find it."

"I didn't *lose* your book," I said to Rebecca. "I know exactly where it is." I had borrowed her book because, like she'd said, I had misplaced mine—temporarily, I hoped, because if it was gone for good, I'd have to pay for it, and textbooks are expensive.

"But I *need* my book," Rebecca said again, in the same loud voice. She didn't calm down until I told her, twice, that I would run home at lunchtime and get it while she was at band practice.

"Meet me at my locker after practice and I'll give you the book," I said. Rebecca didn't know that I had promised to go with Sal when he wrote his driver's test, and I didn't tell her.

Right after I promised Rebecca that I'd get her textbook for her and that she definitely wouldn't have to show up in class looking like she wasn't prepared, I went to Sal's locker, which was halfway down the hall from mine. He wasn't there. I didn't expect him to be. These days he was always in a rush. On top of going to school, he worked practically full time at a McDonald's on the Danforth. And a couple of weeks ago he had started tutoring some of the special ed kids at our school. With all the stuff he was doing, he usually raced through the front door of the school just as the last bell rang. So I scribbled a note to tell him I wouldn't be able to go with him after all because I had to go home and get Rebecca's history text, and I jammed it into one of the vents in the door of his locker. It stuck out just enough that he'd be sure to see it. Then I turned and headed down the hall to homeroom. Teddy smirked at me again as I went by. I ignored him.

Later, when the lunch bell rang, I headed for the closest exit and dashed home. Thirty minutes and one organic peanut-butter-and-honey sandwich later, I was on my way back to school.

But I never got there. Not that afternoon, anyway.

When I got to Gerrard Street, I saw cop cars—cruisers *and* unmarked cars—spread out for about two blocks just east of my school. There were a lot of cops there, too—patrol officers *and* detectives. And a Forensic Identification truck. Uniformed cops were manning barricades that cut off the sidewalk and half the street. When you see something like that, it naturally slows you down. You want to know what's going on.

So I stopped. I looked in one direction and saw that there had been a traffic accident—a bad one. A couple of cars were all smashed up and tangled together. It looked like one of them had been making a left turn and the other one had plowed into it. Little pieces of broken glass sparkled all over the road. There was an ambulance down there, too, so I figured someone must have been hurt. I hoped no one had been killed.

I turned to look in the other direction. I was wondering why the cops had barricaded off so much of the street and why there was another ambulance a whole block away from the car accident. That's when I saw a flash of copper—Rebecca's hair. My heart started to race. What was she doing out here? She was supposed to be at band practice. I looked down at my empty hands and thought about ducking into the school before she saw me.

Too late.

There she was, coming toward me. Rebecca and I had been together for almost a year by then, but still it surprised me when she flung herself at me and wrapped her arms tightly around me, right there out on the street. She was making strange noises. It took a couple of seconds before I figured out what was going on. I pulled away from her just a little so that I could see her face.

I was right. She was crying.

"What's wrong?" I said. I hoped it wasn't about her textbook. "How come you aren't at practice?"

Tears were streaming down her cheeks. "Oh, Mike," she said.

Then, boy, another surprise—there was Riel, a serious expression on his face just like always. When I first saw him, I thought he must be there on account of the car accident. But that didn't make sense. He wasn't with Traffic Services anymore. He'd stopped doing that before he resigned from the cops and started teaching high school. Now that he was back to being a cop, he was with one of the plainclothes units, but not in this neighborhood, so I couldn't figure out what he was doing here. Then I thought he was looking for me on account of something I'd done—or something I hadn't done. Riel is the kind of guy who, when he gets mad about something, wants to deal with it right away. But I couldn't think of a single thing that I'd done to piss him off. Besides, he didn't look mad. But I could tell from his face that something was wrong. He came over to where Rebecca and I were standing.

"I was in the area. I just heard," he said.

That's when it occurred to me that maybe he knew one of the people who had been in that car accident. Maybe it was a teacher from our school. Then I had a terrible thought. Maybe it was Susan. Boy, that would explain why Rebecca was crying.

"I'm sorry to be the one to have to tell you, Mike," he said.

"Tell me what?" I said. I was shaking now. "Is it Susan? Was Susan in an accident?"

"It's Sal," Riel said in a quiet voice.

"Sal?"

"He's dead, Mike."

I laughed. I'm not kidding. I was so surprised and it sounded so ridiculous that I laughed. Then I looked at the tears that were running down Rebecca's face again, and I saw the grim look on Riel's face, and I knew he wasn't kidding.

But I still couldn't believe it.

"What happened?" I said. "Was it the car accident? Did Sal get hit?"

Riel touched my arm to steer me away from all the people. We started walking down the street, away from the police barriers. Rebecca came with us.

"What happened?" I said again.

Riel looked in the window of every restaurant we passed. Finally he opened a door and held it for Rebecca and me. We went inside. The place was practically deserted, probably because everyone was outside watching what was going on. Riel led the way to a booth. He sat on one side. Rebecca and I sat across from him.

"What happened?" I said again. It was really getting to me that he hadn't answered me yet.

"He was stabbed," Riel said.

"*Stabbed*?" What was he talking about? "What do you mean, stabbed?" I said. Rebecca was sniffling next to me, but I was so stunned by what Riel had just said that I didn't think to put my arm around her or even hand her a paper napkin so that she could blow her nose.

"Someone stabbed Sal," Riel said.

"*What?*" I stared at him. Someone had *stabbed* Sal? What kind of sense did that make? Why would anyone stab *Sal*? There had to be some mistake. Sal was a good guy. Sal never got into trouble. "Why would anyone stab Sal?" I said. "What happened?"

"There was a fight," Rebecca said.

"There was some kind of altercation," Riel said, being more careful with his words. "There were a lot of kids out on the street. From what I've heard, some kids were giving another kid a hard time, and Sal got involved."

"What do you mean, he got involved?" I said. "I thought—"

"You thought what?" Riel said.

"He mentioned something about going downtown for the written test for his driver's license," I said. I avoided looking at Rebecca.

"Well, he didn't get there," Riel said. "He got involved in something. Then, some time after that, he was stabbed. But it's not clear yet what happened."

I shook my head. I knew he wasn't making it up. Jeez, why would he make up a thing like that? But I still couldn't believe it.

Riel's phone rang. He answered it, listened for a moment, and said to me, "I have to take this." He got out of the booth and walked to the back of the restaurant where he could have some privacy.

I turned to Rebecca. She reached across me and pulled some napkins from the dispenser on the table.

She wiped her tears, but more kept coming. I had never seen her so upset. Well, who could blame her?

"Do you know what happened?" I said.

"Not exactly," she said. "We were at band practice, and we heard all this commotion out in the hall. Everyone was talking about it. So I came outside."

"You said there was a fight."

"That's what I heard someone say. I heard it was Teddy and his friends. I heard Staci was involved. But that's all I know."

"*Teddy* killed Sal?" I said.

"I don't know," Rebecca said. She wiped more tears.

Riel came back to the booth, but he didn't sit down.

"I'm sorry, Mike, but I have to go," he said. "I don't think much is going to happen at school for the rest of the day. The police are trying to get statements from people who were out on the street when it happened. Why don't you go home? I'll get there as soon as I can."

I nodded. After he left, Rebecca and I just sat there in that booth. We were both stunned. Finally, we got up and went back outside. Riel had said to go home, but we headed back in the direction of the school instead. I don't even know why. Habit, maybe. I kept wondering how Sal had ended up in a fight. Why hadn't he gone straight downtown to take his test like he'd told me he was going to? Had he changed his mind because he didn't want to go alone? Written tests really made him nervous. But, boy, I hated to think that he'd decided not to go because of me, because if he did, then it meant that

I could have prevented what had happened. If I hadn't gone home instead of meeting him like I was supposed to, he would still be alive.

I felt like I was going to throw up. This couldn't be happening. It just couldn't.

Rebecca said something to me when we got close to school, but I wasn't really paying attention.

"Mike," she said. "Did you hear me?"

I nodded, even though I had no idea what she had said. We were in front of the school now. There were kids everywhere, most of them talking.

Rebecca hugged me and then disappeared through the crowd. I sank down onto the curb. My brain kept screaming no, *no, NO!*

I heard bits and pieces of conversation. Everybody was talking about the same thing—what had happened to Sal. After a few minutes, I got up and stumbled over to the nearest small group so I could hear what they were saying. Then I made my way through the whole crowd, listening. But it was hard to get a clear picture of what had happened because there had been a lot of kids outside at lunchtime, and there had been a lot going on. Most of the kids who were talking hadn't actually seen what happened. Most of them had only heard things second- or thirdhand from other kids, so I wasn't even sure if what anyone said was true. But what I pieced together was this: A whole lot of kids from school had gone out onto Gerrard Street that day at lunchtime, like they did every day, to eat and hang out.

It was cool out, but not cold—the perfect kind of day to get a slice of pizza and a pop, whatever, and then hang out on the sidewalk, eating, talking, chilling, horsing around. That's what a lot of kids were doing. So were some kids from another school in the area. A lot of the storekeepers and restaurant owners didn't like that. They were always complaining because sometimes the horsing around got out of control, and they thought that was bad for business.

Riel had said it wasn't clear yet who had done what or said what. He said there were so many people out on the street by the time the cops showed up that the cops weren't sure exactly who had been there when it happened and exactly what everyone had been doing or even exactly where they had been. But the kids I talked to all said what Rebecca had said. They said it had started with Teddy and his friends and that it had involved Staci. They said that Teddy and the rest of them were on the sidewalk on the other side of the street from my school, and Staci came along.

I knew Staci, but I didn't really know her. It was more like I knew who she was. She used to go with Teddy. She'd been with him forever. I never hung out with Teddy. I didn't like him, and I knew he thought I was a loser—first because of my uncle Billy, then because I was living with a teacher at our school who used to be a cop, and now because I was living with a cop. Because of that, I never had much to do with Teddy. So I never got to know Staci. But I had a picture of what she must be like, based on her having been with Teddy so long and based on what the other girls who hung out with Teddy and his friends were like.

But Staci wasn't with Teddy anymore. Rebecca said that Staci had dumped Teddy just before school started. The way Rebecca put it, "She finally opened her eyes." I didn't care one way or the other who Staci went with. Like I said, I didn't know her, and I didn't like Teddy. But Teddy sure cared. I guess he didn't like getting dumped, because he gave Staci a hard time every chance he got. He made fun of her. He talked really loud in the cafeteria and in the halls at school about stuff she used to do with him—at least, stuff he *said* she used to do. Rebecca said she bet most of it was lies. I heard he even e-mailed pictures of her to people. I heard they weren't nice pictures, but I never saw them. And, like I said, I didn't care. I thought, if you spend that much time with a guy like Teddy, you pretty much get what you deserve. At least, that's what I had thought up until the beginning of last week. Since then, I'd been thinking that maybe Staci didn't deserve quite as much as she was getting.

Anyway, it didn't surprise me when I heard what people were telling me out on the street, which was that as soon as Teddy saw Staci coming down the sidewalk at lunchtime, he started giving her a hard time.

And then, people said, Sal got involved. I didn't find anybody who had actually seen it. They had all just heard about it. They all said that Sal was there and that he'd got involved. That didn't surprise me, either.

After that it got kind of fuzzy because, like I said, I couldn't find anyone who had actually seen it. What most people said was this: Teddy and his friends were making so much noise that some of the storeowners and restaurant owners started to look out of their windows. They were losing their patience because there was so much shouting going on and there were so many kids on the sidewalk right outside their businesses. I heard that one storeowner even came out onto the sidewalk to yell at the kids to move on, *move on*, or else he was going to call the police. Maybe if he *had* called the police, things would have turned out differently.

Then there was a big bang and the sound of metal crashing into metal and glass shattering and car horns blowing, and everyone who was standing on the sidewalk on both sides of the street turned to look. And what they saw were those two cars smashed into each other at the next intersection. It wasn't long before they heard sirens, in the distance at first, and then closer and closer. An ambulance showed up. Then a cop car. Then another cop car. Boy, that really got people's attention. Everyone was looking down there to see what had happened. Some people even started to drift in that direction.

Then, a minute or a couple of minutes later, depending on who I was talking to, a woman—nobody seemed to know who she was—ran out of an alley near where Teddy and the rest of them were standing. I heard someone say the woman was wearing a blue smock over her clothes. I heard someone else say she probably worked at the hairdresser's across the street from the school. The woman ran down the street, screaming for the police. A kid who saw her decided to go into the alley to investigate. A couple of other kids followed. One of them must have come out and said something, because more kids went into the alley to see what was going on. One kid threw up. Another kid fumbled in her pocket for her cell phone and punched in 911. But by then the cops were already racing up the street.

As soon as the cops showed up, some of the kids took off. The rest of them milled around until the cops ordered them out of there. I bet 90 percent of those kids watched *CSI* at least once a week. They should have known better. They should have known to stay back and not to touch anything.

The ambulance came. Then more cops. But by then it was too late. Sal was lying in the alley. He was dead before the paramedics got to him. He had been knifed in the chest.

I was shaking all over now. Things would have been different if Sal hadn't called me last night. They would have been different if I hadn't told Rebecca that I'd forgotten her history book and if I hadn't gone home at lunchtime. They would have been different if I'd met Sal and had gone straight downtown with him to take his driver's license test.

Everything would be different.

Sal would still be alive.

CHAPTER THREE

I was standing in a daze outside the school. The whole area was blocked off, and there were cops everywhere. There were lots of people, too, standing, talking, watching. I looked around—I couldn't believe what a nice day it was. It was cool out, definitely jacket weather. The sky was deep blue, with fluffy white clouds, like something a kid would draw in a picture. I bet there were little kids being pushed in swings and whizzing down slides in playgrounds all over the city. I bet there were people smiling while they walked their dogs, grateful for such a nice day because pretty soon it would be getting cold and it would start to get dark in the middle of the afternoon. It just didn't seem right that it was such a bright, sunny day. The way I felt, I wanted it to be pouring rain, with thunder and lightning and the wind whipping the leaves right off the trees.

I had lost track of Rebecca. She'd said something to me when we'd got close to the school, but I hadn't been listening. I didn't know if she had told me where she was going or even if she was coming back. Then I spotted her. She was coming toward me, and she had two of her friends, Luci and Kim, with her. When they got to where I was standing, Rebecca said, "I found them."

I looked blankly at her.

"Kim and Luci," Rebecca said. She looked at me and looped an arm through mine. "I went to see if I could find them, remember?" she said softly.

I had no idea what she was talking about.

"I heard someone say—" she began. Then she shook her head and turned to Kim. "Tell Mike what you told the police," she said.

"You talked to the police?" I said.

"She saw what happened," Rebecca said.

I stared at her. Finally, someone who actually knew something. "You really saw it?"

"I was walking by," Kim said.

"And?"

"I was on my way to the mall. I saw Teddy and the rest of them hanging out on the sidewalk outside the pizza place across the street."

I knew the place she meant. A lot of kids went over there at lunchtime for a slice and a pop. It had the best price around, what it called a student special.

"What were they doing?" I said.

"They were just hanging out, you know, the way those guys do. They were being really loud—that's why I looked over there. They were all crowded around Staci, making fun of her. Teddy was teasing her about hanging out with the retards."

Rebecca winced when she heard that.

"I don't get it," I said. "What did he mean?"

"Staci tutors some of the special ed kids," Kim said.

That surprised me. It was hard to picture someone who'd been so close to Teddy for so long doing something like that. Then I thought, *Maybe that's why Sal got involved.* Even with everything else he was doing, Sal tutored special ed kids, too. Maybe he and Staci had gotten to know each other. It made sense.

"I guess Staci didn't like what Teddy was saying," Kim said. "She hit him."

"Staci hit *Teddy?*" She must have been really mad to do that, especially right in front of all his friends.

"She slapped him," Kim said. "Then the rest of them all started giving her a hard time. Matt"—Matt Levin, another one of Teddy's pals—"started making fun of the way some of the special ed kids walk and talk. He put his arm around Staci, you know, like she was his girlfriend, and he was trying to give her a big slobbery kiss. He was grunting and everything. What a dork! Staci tried to push him away, but he wouldn't let go."

"They're all so ignorant," Rebecca muttered.

"Then I think one of the girls who was there pushed her or something, because it looked like she stumbled." I pictured Sara D. She was one of the Saras who hung out with Teddy. I'd heard that she was trying to get close to Teddy. And I knew how mean she could be. "Or maybe Staci just tripped. It was hard to tell. There were a lot of people out there. That's when Sal went across the street and pulled Matt off Staci and started to walk away with her. He put his arm around her, like he was trying to protect her."

"Sal went across the street?" I said.

Kim nodded.

"So he was on the same side of the street as you when all this was happening, and he saw it, and then he went over there?" When people had told me that he'd gotten involved, I thought maybe he just happened to be walking by when it happened. But, no, Sal had seen what was happening, and he'd gone out of his way to help Staci.

"Yeah," Kim said. "He was with Luci and me on the other side of the street."

I glanced at Luci, who hadn't said anything so far.

"Sal was with you guys?" I said.

Luci nodded.

"We were on our way to Gerrard Square," she said. "Sal caught up with us. He was on his way to the streetcar stop. But he couldn't decide whether he was going to take the streetcar or not."

"What do you mean?" I said, even though I had a pretty good idea. It sounded like he'd decided to postpone the test until I could go with him.

"I think he was planning to go somewhere and then changed his mind," Kim said.

"He definitely changed his mind," Luci said. "There was a streetcar coming. He could have caught it if he'd run. But he didn't. He just shrugged when it went by."

"He said it was an omen," Kim said.

"What did he mean by that?" Rebecca said.

None of them knew. But I did.

"Then he saw Teddy and the rest of them hassling Staci, and he started to go over there," Kim said. "We told him not to." She glanced at Luci. "Didn't we?"

Luci nodded. "So did Miranda," she said.

Miranda was in a couple of Sal's classes. She lived in the same building as Sal. They'd gotten friendly. Sometimes they walked to school or back home together.

"It was stupid," Kim said. "I mean, what was the point of going over there? He was only going to end up getting hassled himself. You know what Teddy's like," she said. "Especially when he's with his friends."

I knew exactly what Teddy was like. My hands curled into fists. My stomach twisted up into a knot. I felt like I wanted to hit something or maybe someone.

"Then what happened?" I said. I had to work at keeping my voice normal or, at least, normal-sounding.

"I already told you," Kim said. "He went across the street and he took Staci by the arm, and I think he said something, only I don't know whether he said it to Staci or to Teddy and Matt and them. Then he started to walk away. He put his arm around Staci. She went with him, but she kept looking back over her shoulder at Teddy. They started to follow her and Sal. There were a lot of them, too, maybe twenty of them—Teddy and Bailey and Matt. I think maybe Jonathan and Steven, but I'm not positive. And some girls, like I said. Annie, I think. And I think maybe Sara D. and Sarah B. Definitely Sara D." Sarah B. was the other Sarah. "There was a whole bunch of people, Mike. They were making a lot of noise. I couldn't hear what they were saying, but someone said that they heard Teddy went ballistic when Sal put his arm around Staci, because he thinks Staci is interested in Sal. The girl who told me that said it looked to her like Teddy was ready for a real fight."

"Then what happened?"

"Then I heard a big bang. I looked to see what it was. We both did, didn't we, Luci?"

Luci nodded.

"Two cars had smashed into each other. Someone must have been hurt, because an ambulance showed up. And—"

"I mean, what happened with Sal?" I said. I didn't care about the car accident.

"I don't know," Kim said. "I didn't see anything. I was looking at the accident. Everyone was looking at the accident. I didn't even know anything had happened to Sal until all of a sudden I saw a woman run down the street to the cops. She looked like she was hysterical. When I looked to see where she'd come from, I saw that there were hardly any kids on the street anymore. Teddy and them were mostly gone. Then a girl came out of the alley. She was crying. So I went across the street to see what was going on."

"You went over there?" I said.

She nodded.

"You waited until Sal was dead, and *then* you went over there?" Boy, I was losing it. I could hear how loud my voice was. I could see the way Rebecca was looking at me—like, what was the matter with me? Luci was looking at me too, with a sort of stunned expression on her face. But I didn't care. I was thinking about all those other kids who had been out there and who, just like Kim and Luci, had seen what was going on. I thought about them just standing there, like they were watching a movie. I thought about not one of them doing anything, except, of course, Sal. "Did you go right into the alley?" I said to Kim. "Did you go and have a good look? Because that's what you like to do, right? You like to just stand there and look."

"I talked to the cops, Mike," Kim said. Her cheeks were pink now and her eyes were watery, but not like she was going to cry. No, she was mad right back at me for talking to her like that. "I told the cops what I saw, okay? It's not my fault what happened to Sal. I didn't do anything."

"You've got that right," I said.

"Mike," Rebecca said.

"You heard her, Rebecca. She didn't do anything. She was there. She saw Staci getting hassled. Then she saw Sal getting hassled. She saw that Teddy wanted a fight."

"I didn't see that part," Kim said. "Someone told me after."

"You should have done something," I said. "Someone should have done something."

"Mike—" Rebecca said.

But I wasn't listening anymore. I was walking away.

CHAPTER FOUR

Riel was home when I got back from school.

"Dave is on his way over," he said. "He wants to talk to you."

"Dave Jones?"

"Yeah. He caught the case."

He meant Sal's case. Dave Jones was a homicide detective.

"Why does he want to talk to me?" I said. "I wasn't there."

"You were Sal's best friend. Maybe there's something you can tell him."

"Yeah, there's something I can tell him," I said. "It was probably Teddy or one of his friends who did it. He should talk to Teddy."

"I know this is hard, Mike. But do me a favor. Don't jump to conclusions. Talk to Dave. Answer his questions. Let him do his job."

Dave Jones showed up at the house fifteen minutes later. Besides being a Homicide detective, he was a friend of Riel's. I knew him, but I didn't know him that well, even though he had been best man at Riel's wedding. He and Riel worked out at the same gym, and they sometimes went to ball games together. He came by the house every now and then, but not as often as he used to before Riel got married and before he went back to being a cop.

Riel showed him into the kitchen and offered him a cup of coffee, which he accepted. While he was still in the room, Dave told me all the regular stuff that cops have to tell kids: that he wanted to ask me some questions but that I didn't have to answer them if I didn't want to, that I could have Riel stay while we talked—it was my right. I told him I didn't need Riel there. I didn't want to see the disapproving look on Riel's face again when I told Dave what I had heard. Riel excused himself and went into the other room.

"I'm sorry about Sal," Dave said. "John tells me the two of you were really close."

I didn't know what to say to that, so I didn't say anything.

Dave pulled a pen and a notebook from his jacket pocket.

"When was the last time you spoke to Sal?" he said.

"What?" What did that have to do with anything? "It was Teddy," I said. "Have you talked to him?"

"Teddy?"

"Teddy Carlin."

"Are you telling me that Teddy Carlin killed Sal?"

"Teddy or one of his loser friends. Or maybe a bunch of them. I wouldn't put it past those guys to swarm Sal.

They're like that. They've done it to other kids." I was thinking about Staci when I said that. "They all hang out down at that construction site where the racetrack used to be." There were *No Trespassing* signs posted everywhere down there, but they didn't keep Teddy out. He and his friends liked to fool around in the half-built houses at night when no one could see them. "I also heard—"

Dave interrupted me.

"Mike, why would Teddy want to hurt Sal?"

I noticed he said *hurt* instead of *kill*.

"Because of Staci." I told him Staci's full name, but he didn't write it down, so I guessed he already knew about her. Maybe he had talked to her. "He already shoved Sal around once because of her."

"You witnessed this, Mike?"

"I sure did."

"Why don't you tell me about that?"

"Staci used to go out with Teddy. But they broke up at the end of the summer. Teddy's been giving her a hard time ever since. So have the kids he hangs out with."

That's the thing that had made me think that Staci didn't deserve the treatment she was getting. It would have been one thing if Teddy was giving her a hard time. After all, she had dumped him. But it wasn't just Teddy. All the kids who hung out with him were in on it, and they could be pretty mean. I found that out at the beginning of last week. I'd gone over to Gerrard Square at lunchtime. I was by myself. Sal had gone to the library to do his homework because he was supposed to be at work that night until midnight. Rebecca was at band practice. I went to the Zellers there to pick up some school stuff. On my way back, I saw a bunch of kids giving someone a hard time. The kids turned out to be all girls. The person they were giving a hard time was Staci.

When guys give other guys a hard time, they usually get physical, and it can be scary if you're the target. People think girls are different, but these ones sure weren't. They were all around Staci. The one who seemed to be leading it all was Sara D. According to Rebecca (Rebecca hears all the gossip that goes around school), Sara D. wanted to go with Teddy, but so far Teddy hadn't asked her out. Maybe that's why she was giving Staci such a hard time that day. Maybe she thought she could score points with Teddy.

I saw Staci in the middle of all those girls. Her face was red. I think she was crying. She tried to push past them, but Sara D. pushed her back. A couple of other girls shoved her too. I saw them. I admit it. But a lot of other people saw them, too. There were kids from my school walking by—on both sides of the street. I felt sorry for Staci. But, like I said, I didn't know her, and the girls who were giving her a hard time were all girls that she used to hang out with when she was with Teddy, so I told myself it was none of my business. Later, I mentioned what had happened to Sal. I said, "Those girls were giving her a really hard time. You wouldn't believe it. Someone should have said something." Sal just gave me a funny look. I didn't figure that out until a couple of days later. *That* was the day I wanted to tell Dave about now—not the day when I should have done something but didn't.

"It happened on Monday," I said.

"You mean, just this past Monday?"

I nodded. "I went up to my locker after school. Sal's locker is down the hall from mine." Because he asked me, I told him which floor and which hallway our lockers were on. I told him our locker numbers, too. Maybe he wanted to check if anyone else had seen what I was going to describe. "When I got there, Teddy was shoving Sal around."

"What do you mean, shoving him around?"

"He was at Sal's locker. He was standing right up close to Sal, and he was jabbing him in the shoulder like this while he talked to him." I showed Dave what I meant. "Other people saw it, too," I said. Most of them were Teddy's friends, except for me—and Alex, who had showed up about the same time I did, but from a different direction.

"What were they talking about?" Dave said.

"Teddy was telling Sal to stay away from Staci. He told Sal that if he didn't stay away from her, he'd be sorry."

"Why was he telling him that? I thought you said Teddy and Staci broke up."

"Staci was the one who broke up with Teddy. I guess Teddy didn't like getting dumped. He's always giving her a hard time about it. I heard the same thing happened today."

"You heard?"

I told him what Kim had said and, because he asked, I gave him Kim's last name. I was pretty sure he was going to want to talk to her.

"Did anything else happen at Sal's locker on Monday?" Dave said.

"Anything else?"

"Did Teddy hit Sal? Did he say anything else? Did Sal say anything? Did they get into a real fight?"

"No," I said. "Teddy jabbed Sal and told him if he didn't leave Staci alone, he'd be sorry."

"And then what?"

"And then Sal walked away."

Dave didn't say anything.

"Don't you get it?" I said. "Teddy didn't want Sal anywhere near Staci. So when Sal went to help Staci, Teddy got mad. Sal was afraid of him."

"Why do you say that?"

I told him what had happened the day before, when Sal and I had come out of school at lunchtime and Sal had seen Teddy and his face had turned white.

"It was Teddy who did it," I said. "It has to be."

"Did anyone else see what you just described, Mike?"

I gave him the names of everyone I could remember.

"But they're all tight with Teddy. They might not tell you anything," I said. "You should try Alex."

"What's Alex's last name?"

"Farmington," I said. "I don't know if he saw the whole thing. But he saw at least part of it. He might have heard something, too."

I wasn't sure if Dave would think Alex was a reliable witness. But he was in school, so he wasn't stupid. If he saw or heard anything, he would probably remember it.

"Might have?" Dave said.

"Well, I didn't talk to him about it. I just noticed he was there."

Dave wrote down Alex's name. Then he said, "What about you, Mike?"

"What about me?"

"John tells me that you've known Sal for a long time."

"Since elementary school. We used to hang out together all the time, me and Sal and Vin."

"Vin?"

"Vincent Taglia," I said. I saw a flicker of recognition in his eyes. It was either from what happened to Robbie Ducharme or what happened at the convenience store. Maybe it was both.

"You say you used to hang out together. You don't anymore?"

"Not the three of us," I said. Vin got in some trouble last fall, and he was in detention for a while. Neither Sal or I saw him for months. Then, after he got out, he got in trouble again. I hadn't seen him since last spring. Neither had Sal. Sal didn't want to have anything to do with him anymore. "Sal and I see each other all the time. Vin goes to a different school. And, anyway, since what happened at the convenience store"—a man and a woman had been shot—"Sal said he was through with Vin."

Dave made a note of that. I wondered if he was going

to want to talk to Vin now. "When was the last time you spoke to Sal?"

"Last night. He phoned me."

"Any special reason?"

Why was he asking that?

"No," I said. I tried to sit still and not squirm. What Sal had said or what I had said, which wasn't much, wasn't going to help the cops find out who had stabbed Sal. It had nothing to do with that. "We just talked about stuff."

Dave looked at me across the table. "What kind of stuff?"

"School stuff. Nothing important." At least, nothing that was important to anyone but me.

"When was the last time you saw him?"

"Yesterday at school."

"You didn't see him today?"

"No."

"I understand that you and Sal usually had lunch together."

"We did if he wasn't tutoring."

"Was he tutoring today?"

"No."

"But you didn't have lunch with him today?"

"No."

"Any particular reason why not?"

Cops. They reminded me of that song on *Sesame Street*—one of these things is not like the others, one of these things just doesn't belong. They were always looking for what was different, always had an eye out for the broken pattern.

"I had to come home to get something," I said. Then, because he was being such a cop now and because cops liked to check every single detail, I added, "A textbook. History."

"Was there any trouble between you and Sal?" he said.

"What?" I couldn't believe he was asking me that. "He's my friend!"

"Do you remember what time it was when you got home at lunchtime today, Mike?"

"I don't know. Ten after twelve, maybe quarter after. Why are you—?"

"Anyone see you come into the house?"

"I don't know. I don't remember. There were people on the street, but—"

"You remember anyone in particular?"

"No. Just people. Some parents walking little kids."

"What time did you leave the house to go back to school?"

I was getting tense now. "Maybe twenty minutes after that. I had a sandwich first."

"Anybody see you leave the house?"

"I don't know."

"What did you do after you left the house?"

"I went back to school."

"Did you make any stops on the way?"

"No."

"Did you run into anyone you know on the way?

Anyone who can say where you were at the time Sal died?"

"No," I said again. I was mad now. "You're acting like you think *I* did it."

"I'm just asking questions, Mike. It's my job."

"I didn't kill him."

He looked at me.

"Did Sal ever say anything to you about any problems he might have been having with anyone? Was anyone giving him a hard time?"

"Besides Teddy, you mean?"

"Yes. Besides Teddy."

"No."

"Did he ever tell you that anyone had threatened him, anything like that?"

"No. Just Teddy."

Then he dropped a bomb on me.

"Mike, did you ever see Sal with a weapon of any kind?" he said.

"*What?*"

He repeated the question, as if it were no big deal, as if it were the kind of question that people asked each other all the time, the way they ask, *How are you?*

"What kind of weapon?"

"Any kind of weapon." In other words, he wasn't going to tell me.

"No," I said.

"Did he ever mention anything to you about owning a weapon?"

"No," I said again. "Sal's not that kind of person. Why?"

He didn't answer that question either. Cops never tell you anything. Riel says it's because they don't want to influence the people they're interviewing in any way and, also, they don't want regular people to find out exactly what they know and what they don't know until they have their case together.

"Is there anything else you want to tell me about Sal?" he said, still in that neutral tone.

I shook my head. He closed his notebook.

"Okay, Mike," he said. "I'll let you know if I need to talk to you again."

After he left, Riel came into the kitchen. He must have seen how I was feeling, because he said, "He's a good cop, Mike. He knows what he's doing."

CHAPTER FIVE

The morning after Sal died, I got out of bed, as usual. I got dressed and went downstairs to the kitchen, as usual. And, as usual, Riel had already been up for ages. He was sitting at the kitchen table, working on a mug of black coffee, and he had the newspaper open in front of him. Something that wasn't usual: I felt like punching my fist through a wall. Because it wasn't right that I was doing the all the regular things as if nothing had happened, when something *had* happened. Someone had killed Sal. And now Riel was sitting there with his coffee and reading about it in the newspaper. The article wasn't long. It didn't say much except who Sal was and where he went to school and where he was killed. And that he'd been found lying in that alley by a hairdresser who had stepped out back to have a smoke.

"Are you okay, Mike?" Riel said.

What kind of question was that?

"You look like you didn't get much sleep," he said.

He had that right.

Something else that wasn't usual:

"Are you hungry?" Riel said, getting up from the

table and going to the cupboard. "You want something to eat? How about some cornflakes?"

Other than the first couple of days I had lived with him, Riel never got my breakfast for me. If I wanted juice or milk, I knew where to find it. Same with cereal and toast.

"I'm okay," I said.

"You have to eat, Mike."

"I'm not hungry."

Riel hesitated, one hand on the fridge door, trying to decide how much to push. Finally he sat down at the table again.

"You're not working today, are you?"

I had a part-time job stocking shelves at a grocery store, not the small store where I used to work, but a big supermarket that was open 24/7.

"No," I said.

"When I get home, we should go and see Sal's parents. Okay?"

Sal's parents. Boy, I wasn't looking forward to that. Sal was an only child. I couldn't begin to imagine how his mother and father were feeling right now.

Riel glanced at his watch. "Look, I'm sorry. If I could stay, I would. But I have to get to work." He gulped down the last of his coffee and stood up. "Get yourself something to eat, Mike. It'll make you feel better. And go to school, okay? They'll probably have some grief counselors there. If you want to, you can talk to someone."

Talk to a stranger? About Sal? What was I supposed

to say about Sal to someone who didn't even know him?

I went to school. Rebecca was waiting for me at my locker. She hugged me. "Did they find out who did it yet?" she said.

"They don't even know why it happened."

"I heard the cops talked to Teddy."

Well, finally. "Did they arrest him?"

"I don't think so. I saw him this morning when I got to school."

What was going on? Why was Teddy still walking around? Why didn't they have him locked up somewhere? Why hadn't they—

The bell rang.

"Mike?" Rebecca said gently. The look on her face told me she was going to say something that she didn't want to. I felt myself tense up. "Don't get mad," she said. "But I was wondering about my history book."

Right.

I opened my locker and took out her book. I felt like ripping it into a million pieces. Stupid book! I handed it to her without a word. But I didn't look at her because I had spotted Teddy at the end of the hall. Seeing him there was bad enough. What made it worse was that he was talking to Miranda. She was supposed to be a friend of Sal's. What was she doing with Teddy? Didn't she realize what he had done? Wait a minute—maybe she did.

Maybe that's what she was talking about, because Teddy started to shake his head, like he was denying something. Miranda kept talking to him, and Teddy kept shaking his head. If I'd been Miranda, I would have walked away by now. I wouldn't have wasted my breath on him.

I turned my back to them and got the stuff I needed out of my locker. Rebecca kissed me on the cheek, and we split up. I went to homeroom. I listened to the announcements. It was just like Riel had said—there were people at school that we could talk to if we wanted to. People who helped people deal with situations like this—or so they said.

Everywhere I went that day, people were talking about what had happened. Lots of kids, especially girls who were all teary-eyed, said what a great guy Sal was. They were right about that. Sal was quiet and polite. He worked hard at keeping his grades up, even with all the hours he was putting in at his job. All of his teachers respected him for that—and for tutoring those special ed kids. When he told me he had signed up for that, I asked him if he was crazy.

"You hardly have any time to hang out as it is," I said.

He just shrugged. "I like to help people, Mike," he'd said. "It makes me feel good."

Me—I liked to hang out and relax, preferably with Rebecca. That made me feel good.

Sal got along great at work, too. They liked him so much that over the summer he had been promoted to shift manager. He never got into trouble anymore and, to be honest, when we were younger and the three of us used to hang out together—Vin and Sal and me—he never got into half the trouble that Vin and I did. He was a good guy. He was nice to everyone.

My stomach clenched up when I got to math class. Sal sat beside me in math. But for the first time this year, his desk was empty. Mr. Tran, who was my math teacher for the second year in a row, avoided looking at it. I couldn't take my eyes off it.

After math I had French. I sat behind a couple of girls who spent the time before the bell talking about the awful thing that had happened and what a nice guy they thought Sal was. One of them said maybe Sal was too nice and that he should have known better than to defend someone who was as trashy as Staci. Didn't he know what everyone was saying about her, didn't he know what Teddy could be like?

I tapped her on the shoulder. "You say he was a nice guy and then you dump on him for acting nice," I said.

The girl—her name was Melissa—glared at me for eavesdropping. Then she said, "If you're going to go up against Teddy, you should at least do it over something that matters."

"You don't know what you're talking about," I said. I guess my voice was pretty loud because the buzz in the classroom—you know, all the kids talking before the teacher walks in—all of a sudden stopped. "You didn't even know him," I said.

As I was saying that, Monsieur Tétrault walked in.

He glanced around the room and then focused in on the two girls and me.

"*Est-ce qu'il y a un problème?*" he said.

The two girls faced front. I shook my head, looked down at my desk, and didn't say another word, not even when Monsieur Tétrault asked me a question. Who even cared about French, especially when someone you knew had just died? Especially when . . .

I shouldn't have bailed on Sal. I should have met him like I'd promised. I should have gone downtown with him. I should have just dealt with it.

I caught up with Rebecca in the cafeteria at lunchtime, like always—well, except that Sal wasn't there, too. We sat near the back, at one of the smaller tables. Kim and Luci came over and looked like they were going to sit down. But I glowered at Kim, and she hesitated, like she couldn't decide what to do. Rebecca looked at me and then at Kim. For a minute I thought she was going to tell them to join us, but she didn't. Kim and Luci went to sit someplace else.

Rebecca and I just sat there. We didn't eat, even though Rebecca had brought a lunch and I had bought a slice of pizza. We didn't talk, either. Rebecca held one of my hands.

I heard someone laughing at a table close to the one we were sitting at. It was a loud, annoying laugh, like a jackass braying. I glanced over Rebecca's shoulder. The laughter was coming from Teddy's table, which was twice the size of the one we were at. All his friends were sitting with him. They were laughing and horsing around and being five times louder than anyone else—as usual. It was like they had to be loud so that everyone would look at them and see what a great time they were having and think how cool they were—at least, that's what it felt like.

Then I heard someone at Teddy's table—I'm not even sure who it was—say Staci's name. Everyone laughed again, louder this time.

That did it.

I stood up.

Rebecca grabbed my hand.

"Mike," she said. Her voice was soft, like she was warning me about something.

I shook free of her and pushed my way through the chairs to where Teddy and his friends were sitting. I squeezed past people and between tables until I was standing over Teddy, who had curly black hair and sharp black eyes and was laughing harder than anyone at whatever it was that one of his jackass friends had said. I stood so close to him that he had to crane his neck to look at up me.

"What?" he said, annoyed, like he was trying to get a tan and I was blocking the sun. He sounded pissy and superior all at the same time, and all of a sudden I could imagine how it had happened. I could imagine that smug look on his face as he said something smart-assed about Staci and made fun of the kids she tutored and the way they talked. I could imagine him saying stuff about Staci, too. He always did. I remembered how he had jabbed Sal up at his locker and told him to stay away from Staci or he'd be sorry, and I could imagine the hard time he'd given Sal out there on the street, too, when Sal had waded into the crowd and had taken Staci by the arm. I could see it playing out right in front of my eyes, like a video. And that's when I did it.

I grabbed the front of Teddy's T-shirt with both hands and wrenched him to his feet. I heard his chair legs squeal against the tiled floor. I saw the look of surprise in his eyes as I yanked him toward me. I saw the shock of pain as my fist smashed into his face. Then more chairs shrieked against the tile, and the guys who were sitting around the table jumped up and a couple of them, it felt like, grabbed me from behind and pinned my arms to my sides and Teddy stepped into me, his nose bleeding, his hands curling into fists. Then I saw a flash of coppery hair. Rebecca. She was trying to get between Teddy and me. But someone—I think it was Sara D., but I'm not positive—pushed Rebecca. She lurched backward, tripped over something—I didn't see what— and crashed to the floor.

That did it.

I started thrashing around, trying to wrestle free of Teddy's buddies so that I could swing at Teddy again. Then I spotted Mr. Gianneris, one of the school's vice principals, wading through chairs and tables and kids toward us.

Teddy nodded at the guys who had pinned my arms

at my sides, and they let me go. I went over to Rebecca, who was back on her feet and glowering at Sara D. Teddy's two friends, the ones who had been holding me, retreated before Mr. Gianneris reached us, but Teddy stayed exactly where he was, blood running from his nose down over his chin and dripping onto his shirt. Boy, did that get Mr. Gianneris's attention.

"What's going on here?" he said, looking from Teddy to me and back to Teddy again.

I was sure Teddy was going to rat me out. Instead, he said, "I tripped. I hit the table on the way down."

Mr. Gianneris took a good look at Teddy's face. He looked at Teddy's friends. He looked around at all the other kids who might have seen what had happened. Then he zeroed in on Rebecca. Sweet, honest Rebecca.

"Is that what happened?" Mr. Gianneris asked her.

Rebecca glanced at me. So did Mr. Gianneris.

"I asked *you*, Rebecca. I didn't ask Mike," he said.

I didn't care whether she told him the truth or not. If you hit another kid, it's an automatic suspension. Depending on how hard you hit him and how much damage you do, it could even be an expulsion. But so what? The way I was feeling—being here, knowing how many people had seen what had happened, knowing that none of them had done anything—I didn't care if they threw me out for good and I never saw any of them ever again. Well, except for Rebecca.

"It's like Teddy said," Rebecca said finally. "He tripped and fell."

Mr. Gianneris peered into her eyes. So did I, and was I ever surprised at how convincing she looked. I didn't know Rebecca was such a good liar.

Mr. Gianneris turned to Sara D., who glanced at Teddy and said she didn't know what had happened, she'd been looking the other way. So did everyone else at Teddy's table. They all lied. They all said exactly what Teddy wanted them to say. I bet they'd lied to the cops, too.

"Fine," Mr. Gianneris said, but you could tell that he didn't think it was fine at all. He pulled a handkerchief out of his pocket and handed it to Teddy. "Is it broken?"

"I don't think so," Teddy said. He used the handkerchief to wipe away the blood.

"Still, you should have it looked at," he said. "Is anyone home at your house?"

"My mother. She works nights."

"Go to the office," Mr. Gianneris said. "Have Ms. Loomis call your mother." Then he turned to me. "Report to my office, Mike. Stay there until I get there."

» » »

Teddy was sitting on a bench in the office when I got there. Someone—probably Ms. Loomis—had pressed a wad of tissues into his hand. The bleeding didn't look so bad now. I wasn't sure how I felt about that.

"I'm supposed to wait for Mr. Gianneris in his office," I told Ms. Loomis. She waved me back behind the counter. I went down the narrow corridor to Mr.

Gianneris's office and sat down on one of the chairs opposite his desk.

I heard Mr. Gianneris's voice in the outer office a few minutes later. He asked Teddy how he was. Teddy said the bleeding had stopped and asked if he could go back to the cafeteria. Mr. Gianneris said no, he had to wait for his mother. He told Ms. Loomis to let him know the minute she showed up. Then he came into his office, closed the door, and sat down at his desk. He leaned back in his chair, his fingertips pressed together, and stared at me for a long time before he finally said, "I'm sorry about what happened to Sal. We all are."

I didn't say anything.

"You know we have grief counselors in the school today, don't you, Mike?" he said. "Did you talk to them?"

I shook my head.

"These are people who understand what you're going through, Mike. A lot of students have seen them today."

A *lot* of students? I wondered who. Who could possibly have felt even close to what I felt about what had happened?

"Are you sure you don't want to talk to one of them, Mike?"

"Yeah," I said. "I'm sure." Because, when you got right down to it, what would I say? What *could* I say?

Mr. Gianneris studied me for a few moments. "I know what the situation was out there yesterday. I know how close you and Sal were," he said. "And I know you're probably thinking about him. So I'm going to let this go—this time. And I'm going to trust that you'll let the police do their jobs. You hear what I'm saying, Mike?"

I nodded. I knew he was trying to be nice and that I should be grateful. But I wasn't. Not at all.

"Okay," Mr. Gianneris said. "You're excused."

CHAPTER SIX

Riel didn't get home until after I had made myself some supper. He parked out front instead of in the driveway and came into the house just long enough to say, "I'm sorry, I got tied up at work. Come on, let's go and see Sal's parents."

"Is there anything new?" I said as I followed him out of the house. "Did they find out anything yet?"

"They did the autopsy this morning," Riel said. "But that's all I know so far."

The autopsy. I felt sick just thinking about it. I'd seen autopsies on TV. I didn't want to think about Sal lying on a stainless steel table in some pathologist's lab with Dave Jones watching while the pathologist cut Sal open and examined him. I didn't want to think about the two of them talking about him—the pathologist telling Dave how it had happened and Dave asking questions that might help him with the case. Doing their jobs, the two of them. Doing it with Sal lying there.

"Can't you ask Dave what's going on?"

"I did, Mike."

"Can't you help him? You used to be in Homicide.

Everyone said you were good. And you know the school. You know most of the kids. Why can't you do something?"

"It's not my job, Mike."

Right. He was tied up with other more important stuff, like local robberies and break-and-enters. Since he'd gone back to being a cop, he was always grumbling about how the city was going downhill, how drug addicts were stealing bikes and selling them for five or ten bucks and how so-called reputable bike stores were reselling the bikes as used for a hundred dollars or more. Or he was grousing about youth crime, like purse snatching and shoplifting, which was the main kind of crime he was looking into these days. Or vandalism and graffiti at construction sites around town, like that one down where the racetrack used to be, where kids like Teddy like to hang out. One night during the summer, Riel had even asked Susan what the world was coming to. It turned out someone had stolen some trees and flowers that some homeowner had just planted on his property. Riel got assigned to look into that.

"The funeral is going to be on Monday," Riel said. "Sal's parents want to give some of their relatives a chance to get here." Sal's parents were from Guatemala. Sal still had relatives there. He also had relatives in the United States and in a few other countries. "Come on, we'd better get going. I know Sal's parents will want to see you. I know it'll mean a lot to them."

I'd been thinking about Sal's parents on and off all

day. I didn't know how I could face them. It just kept eating at me and eating at me how it never would have happened if I hadn't bailed on Sal at lunchtime. But I knew that going over there was the right thing to do, no matter what.

» » »

The drive to Sal's place didn't take long—maybe ten minutes. We were quiet on the way. Maybe Riel wasn't in the mood to talk. Or maybe he sensed that I wasn't. Either way, I was grateful.

Sal's parents lived in an apartment in a low-rise building with one of Sal's aunts. They used to have their own house, but they had to give that up when Sal's father got sick and Sal's mother's job went from being full-time to being part-time. But a couple of months ago, Sal's mother had found another job—a really good one. Sal had told me they were going to stay with his aunt until his mother had put in six months and they were all sure her new job was going to work out. Then they were going to get their own place again, and Sal was going to go back to working part-time instead of nearly full-time. He'd been excited about that.

My stomach was doing backflips as we approached the apartment building. Riel pressed the buzzer on the panel next to the main door. When someone answered— I'm pretty sure it was Sal's aunt—he identified himself and said that I was with him. We were buzzed through.

Sal's aunt answered the apartment door when Riel knocked. Riel said something to her in Spanish. He spoke the language pretty well, but I didn't understand a word of what he said to her. When Sal's aunt stepped aside to let us in, I saw that there were a lot of people crammed into the living room and dining room. There were people in the kitchen, too, mostly women, almost all of them speaking Spanish. Riel nudged me into the living room, where Sal's parents were sitting side by side on the sofa. Sal's mother got up when she saw us. She spoke to Riel in Spanish. Then she threw her arms around me and hugged me tightly and told me how glad she was to see me. When I told her how sorry I was about what had happened, she started to cry. She hung onto me for another few moments. Sal's dad didn't look at me. He didn't look at anyone. He just sat there on the couch with a blank look on his face, like maybe he didn't even realize what was going on. He'd had some kind of mental breakdown. He'd been really sick, and it didn't look like he had gotten better yet.

After Sal's mother let me go, I looked around to see who else had come. Mostly they were people I didn't know, friends of Sal's parents, I guess. But I spotted a couple of teachers and, oh boy, coming out of the kitchen with a tray of cups and saucers, Imogen. She had gone out with Sal last winter and spring. She'd been going out with him when Sal had seen three guys run out of a convenience store where the owner and his wife had just been shot. Imogen had made plenty of trouble for me over that. I guess she knew how I felt about her being there, because when she saw me, she almost dropped the tray she was carrying. But she recovered and made it to the dining room table. She looked at me again as she started taking cups and saucers off the tray and setting them onto the table, only now she didn't look startled. Now she looked like she wished I would get lost. Then a teacher went to the table to get some coffee, and he said something to Imogen, and she nodded and handed him a cup. She didn't look at me again the rest of the time I was there. She didn't come over to talk to me, either, which was fine with me.

Riel and I stayed for about half an hour. Before we left, Riel went over to Sal's mother again and spoke to her again in Spanish. Then I heard him say, "Mike would be honored, wouldn't you, Mike?"

I gave him a blank look. Honored about what?

"Maria wants you to be one of the pallbearers at the funeral," Riel said.

I turned to Sal's mother. There were tears in her eyes, but she was smiling at me anyway. She said, "It would mean a lot to his father and to me."

"Sure," I said. "Sure, okay." Inside I was thinking about what it would be like to be right there beside the casket, knowing that Sal was inside.

"I also asked Vincent," his mother said.

"You asked Vin?" I said.

Sal's mother nodded.

Now I was confused. As far as I knew, Sal and Vin

hadn't talked to each other in nearly a year, ever since Robbie Ducharme had died and Vin had been charged in the case. And then there was that thing with the convenience store. Maybe Sal's mother didn't know how Sal felt about Vin.

"He came here this morning," Sal's mother said.

"*Vin?*" I said, like I couldn't believe he would do something like that. Well, I couldn't.

"The three of you were friends for such a long time," she said. "So I asked him. I think Salvatore would like to know his old friends were there for him. Old friends are the most important kind, no?"

"Sure," I said. But my insides felt all twisted up. Boy, I wished things were different.

Riel was quiet for a few minutes after we got to the car, but I was pretty sure I knew what he was thinking about. Finally he said, "When was the last time you saw Vin?"

Yeah, I was right.

"A couple of months ago, I guess. Why?" As if I didn't already know the answer. Riel didn't approve of Vin. Vin got into too much trouble, and lately most of it was serious.

"Just wondering," he said. "Do you know if Sal had seen him lately?"

"I doubt it," I said. It didn't seem likely to me, given how Sal felt about Vin. "Why?" As if I didn't already know the answer to that one, either.

"Just wondering," Riel said again.

Right. He would probably wonder his way over to the telephone later to call Dave, who, if he hadn't already done it, would knock on Vin's door and ask him some questions.

» » »

I had to work the next day, and I was glad. It gave me something to do. I wouldn't have to think about Sal. The store I worked at was one of those big ones that's open twenty-four hours a day, seven days a week. I usually worked a couple of four-hour shifts, five to nine, during the week and one or two longer shifts on either Saturday or Sunday or, every once in a while, on both days. Today I was working eight to four thirty. My job was stocking the shelves. It was easy work. Well, it was easy for most people. I was pushing a skid of canned and creamed corn to the canned vegetable aisle when I heard the floor manager chewing someone out.

"No, no, no," he was saying. "Look at the pictures, for Pete's sake. Carrots. Peas. Beans. They're *vegetables*. And what are you putting on the shelf? Cans of pineapple. Pineapple is a *fruit*."

The guy he was yelling at, a beefy guy with washed-out blond hair and a twitchy left leg that never seemed to stop moving, was standing in the middle of the aisle with his shoulders hunched over and his head down, like he was afraid the floor manager was going to start lobbing those cans of pineapple at him. It was Alex Farmington, one of the kids from school.

"Do you understand what I'm telling you, Alex?" the floor manager, Mr. Geordi, said.

"Barry told me to take these cans and fill the hole in aisle six," Alex said. He glanced up at the big sign that hung over the middle of the aisle. It had the aisle number on it—six—plus what was in the aisle: canned fruit, canned vegetables, soups, crackers, and cookies.

"He meant the hole in the *fruit* section," Mr. Geordi said, sounding even more exasperated, although he was trying to keep his voice down. I couldn't tell if that was because he was trying to stay calm so that Alex didn't get even more rattled, or if he just didn't want any of the customers to hear him yelling at one of the disabled employees. The company that owned the store made a big deal of its hiring policy. Every store in the whole chain had a couple of employees who were disabled in some way. Maybe the company did it because they were really nice, or maybe they did it because they wanted their customers to think they really cared. I don't know. But right now it looked like Mr. Geordi couldn't believe that he was standing there explaining the difference between pineapple and corn to one of his workers. "This is the vegetable section. Get these cans out of here and put them where they belong. You think you can do that, Alex?"

Alex nodded.

"Good," Mr. Geordi said. It came out sounding kind of sarcastic, and he was muttering to himself when he went past me a few seconds later. Most people in the store were nice to Alex. Not Mr. Geordi. He was mostly impatient. But he was that way with everyone. I thought that maybe being impatient with Alex was his way of not treating him differently. Rebecca didn't agree. When I told her about Mr. Geordi and Alex, she said, "I bet he wouldn't talk to Alex like that if he was missing a leg or if he was blind. Some people are so backward about intellectual disabilities, they're practically medieval."

Alex started taking the cans of pineapple off the shelf one by one and putting them back into the cartons he had just taken them out of. I pushed my skid down to him. When he was hired, he was paired with me for a couple of shifts so that I could show him what he was supposed to do and the right way to do it. He seemed really nervous, like he was afraid all the time that he was going to make a mistake. When I first met him, I didn't want to ask him what was wrong with him—I thought it would be rude or he'd take it the wrong way. But he came right out and told me. He said he'd been in an accident, something to do with a tractor, and that he'd been unconscious for nearly a month. He said when he woke up, he had to learn to do everything all over again—walk, talk, feed himself. Everything. I couldn't even imagine what that must have been like. He was kind of uncoordinated, he worked slowly, and his left leg was always twitching. But he sure tried hard.

"Let me give you a hand, Alex," I said.

He brightened up when he saw me. "It's okay, Mike," he said. "I can do it."

"Yeah, but your pineapple is where my corn is supposed to be and my shift ends in fifteen minutes. I don't want to have to work late if I don't have to."

It was the wrong thing to say. His face turned red, like now he was afraid that *I* was going to get mad.

"It's no big deal," I said. "It'll just go faster if we do it together."

I grabbed the cans four at a time and dumped them into the cartons. Alex continued on doing things his way—slow and deliberate, one can at a time. While I worked, I said, "Did the cops talk to you, Alex?"

"The cops?" he said. "What about?"

"About what happened at school. You know, the kid who got killed."

"I didn't see anything," Alex said. "I was inside the school."

"But did they talk to you about something that happened earlier in the week, on Monday?"

He looked confused. I wondered if he had seen Teddy jab Sal after all. Or, if he had, I wondered if he remembered.

"No," he said. "The cops didn't talk to me. I didn't see anything."

Finally the shelf space I needed was empty, and Alex pushed his cartons of pineapple down to the other end of the aisle. He had only got half of them unpacked and into the right place by the time I had finished unpacking my skid, which had twice as many cans on it. I called good-bye to him and headed back to the storeroom, where I swiped my employee card to sign out. I pushed open the door to the employee entrance, stepped out into the parking lot behind the store, and just about collided with Bailey Zackery. Kim had said that Bailey had been with Teddy when Teddy started hassling Staci. I wondered what he was doing here. I sure hoped the store hadn't hired him, because I didn't think I could stand to work side by side with someone who had been in on giving Sal a hard time, someone who might even have been involved in what happened or who might know something but wasn't telling the cops.

We looked at each other for a few seconds. Then I walked past him and didn't look back.

Riel was waiting for me in the parking lot. We drove to the funeral parlor where they had Sal's coffin. Riel made me sign the visitors' book, and we went in. People were coming and going. In between, they went up to Sal's parents, who were sitting up near the coffin, and talked to them and hugged them. The whole time I was there, I felt like I couldn't breathe. I kept looking at the coffin and thinking about what was inside. I hate to say it, because I felt bad for Sal's parents, but I was glad to get out of there.

That night I went over to Rebecca's. We watched a couple of movies. Rebecca didn't press me to talk. She seemed to understand how I felt. Maybe she felt the same way. Rebecca hadn't known Sal for anywhere near as long as I had, but she had liked him a lot.

CHAPTER SEVEN

On Sunday Rebecca had to go with her parents to see her grandparents up in Muskoka. I tried to do some homework, but I couldn't concentrate. I decided to take a walk, and you know where I ended up? At Vin's house.

"Mike," his mother said when she answered the door. "What a surprise!" She looked surprised, too, like she had just opened the fridge to get a glass of milk and had found a live cow inside. "I was very sorry to hear about Sal. I know Vincent was, too."

"Is he here?" I said.

She shook her head. "He went to the library."

"The library?" Vin went a lot of places. The library wasn't one of them.

His mother must have known it, too, because she smiled. "He actually seems to like the school he's going to."

I had heard that he was going to a place called the Downtown Academy. It was an alternative school for kids who were having trouble in regular school.

"He's working on a project with some other kids," she said. She told me which library he'd gone to. It was the big one right downtown.

I didn't plan to go there. Vin was busy. He was with other people. Besides, I hadn't seen him since the spring. But once I started walking, I found myself headed across the viaduct, then over to Yonge Street, where I turned and walked up one block. The library was huge, with five different floors filled with bookshelves and computers and big tables where people could sit and work, and a big open space in the middle of each floor where the stairs and the elevator were and where you could look all the way down and all the way up. I wandered around floor after floor. It wasn't until I was on the top floor, looking down, that I spotted Vin. He was on the main floor with three other guys. They all had backpacks, and it looked like they were getting ready to leave. I was trying to decide if I'd be able to catch him if I ran down all five flights of stairs. I was also trying to decide if I even wanted to—it had been a long time—when he looked up and spotted me. He smiled and waved, and it didn't feel like any time had passed at all since we'd seen each other. He gestured for me to come down to where he was.

The three other guys were still with him when I got back down to the main floor.

"Hey, Mikey!" Vin said. "What are you doing here?"

"I heard you were here," I said. The three other guys didn't say anything. They just looked at me like they were wondering who I was. One of them said something to Vin. Then Vin said, "I'll catch up with you later," and the three guys looked at me again and then turned and walked away.

"It's okay," I said. "I mean, if you've got plans—" I hadn't seen him in months. I hadn't even tried to see him. But it felt weird to know that he had a whole bunch of new friends.

"Yeah, I got plans," Vin said with a grin. "I plan to get something to eat and catch up with an old friend. Come on."

As we walked away from the library, his face got more serious.

"I heard about Sal," he said.

I got that same feeling I'd had at the funeral home, like I couldn't breathe.

"Are you okay, Mikey?" Vin said.

I nodded, even though my heart was pounding and I felt like I was sweating all over. Vin put a hand on my shoulder and squeezed it.

We walked to a restaurant a couple of blocks from the library. It turned out that it was right near Vin's school. As soon as we walked in, one of the waitresses smiled at Vin like she not only knew him but she was glad to see him. Vin smiled back. He led me to a booth in the back. The waitress followed us. She said, "Hey, Vincent. You want your regular, or are you going to be adventurous for a change?"

"I'll go for the tried and true," Vin said. He nodded at me. "This is my friend Mike. Mike, this is Linzey."

Linzey glanced at me, but just barely. She seemed a lot more interested in Vin.

"They do a great bacon cheeseburger here, Mike,"

Vin said. "And an excellent chocolate milkshake."

For some reason, the thought of food made me feel queasy. "Just a Coke for me," I said.

Linzey nodded, smiled at Vin again, and went to get our order.

"She's great, huh?" Vin said. "She's the same age as us."

"You know her from school?" I said.

Vin shook his head. "She goes to an alternative school, but not the same one as me. She goes to a school where all the kids are these weird creative types. She's really smart, Mike. Really interesting, too. Her dad owns this place. She works here part-time. It's why I come here." He grinned again. "So . . ." He looked across the table at me. "How are you doing, Mikey?"

"Okay, I guess," I said. "You?"

"I went to see Sal's parents."

"I know," I said. "His mom told me."

"I felt pretty bad," Vin said. "They were really busted up. Sal's mom asked me to help at the funeral."

"It was nice of you to go over there," I said. "You know, considering."

"Considering?" Vin said.

"You know. Considering that you and Sal weren't exactly friends anymore."

Vin shrugged. "We were getting along okay."

"What do you mean?" The way he'd said it, it sounded like he and Sal had been hanging out together. But that couldn't be right.

"He came over to my house a couple of months ago,"

Vin said. He must have caught the surprise on my face because then he said, "I guess he didn't tell you, huh?"

"No."

Linzey came back with a Coke for me and a chocolate milkshake for Vin. He thanked her when she put it down in front of him, which told me how much he liked her. Vin usually didn't waste his breath saying thank you—at least, the old Vin didn't. After Linzey went to take an order from another table, Vin said, "He called me up, then he came over."

"But I thought—" I stopped. I couldn't think of a way to put it that wouldn't sound bad.

"You thought he hated my guts after what happened at that convenience store," Vin said. He grinned again. It took a lot to put Vin in a bad mood. "I thought so, too. But he called me and asked if he could come over. I said sure, if he wanted to. But don't get the wrong idea, Mike. He didn't apologize to me or anything. Not that he had anything to apologize for. He didn't do anything wrong. He never did. He just came over, and we talked for a while." He shook his head again. "I still can't believe he's dead."

Dead.

The word shook me. Sal was dead.

Gone.

Forever.

"Why did he want to see you?" I said.

Vin sucked up some of his chocolate milkshake. "Old time's sake, I guess."

"Yeah? What did you talk about?"

Vin didn't answer. It was like he hadn't heard me. Instead, he was focused on something behind me. I turned and saw Linzey leaning into a booth to pick up dirty dishes. Her back was to us, and you could see how tight her jeans were.

"Vin," I said, louder now, like I was talking to someone with a hearing problem. "What did you and Sal talk about?"

Vin's eyes followed Linzey as she carried a tray-load of dirty dishes back into the kitchen. Then he shifted his attention back to me.

"Stuff," he said. "His job. What I was up to. Why?"

"I'm just surprised, that's all," I said.

Linzey came back to the table. This time she was carrying a plate with a bacon cheeseburger on it, a huge pile of skinny French fries, and a little paper cup of coleslaw. She set it down in front of Vin and said, "*Bon appétit*, Vincent."

"I think she likes me," Vin said after she had gone.

"She sounds like your mom," I said. "The way she calls you Vincent."

"Everyone calls me Vincent now, Mike. I like it." He reached for the ketchup and started to squirt it all over his fries.

"You want me to call you Vincent?" I said.

"It's up to you. You've known me since kindergarten. You're used to it being different. The people who call me Vincent, mostly they're people who haven't known me long. They're new people in my life, people I get to start all over with, people who maybe so far don't think I'm a jerk."

"I can call you Vincent if you want," I said.

He shrugged, like it didn't make any difference to him one way or the other.

"So Sal came over to your house and you guys talked, and that was it?" I said.

Vin squeezed some mustard and ketchup onto his hamburger and some vinegar onto his fries.

"I saw him a couple of times after that," he said. He picked up the burger and took a huge bite. "I guess he didn't tell you that either, huh?"

"No," I said. I didn't get it. Sal had been so mad at Vin about what happened at the convenience store. He'd told me Vin wasn't his friend anymore. And then he'd gone over to Vin's house—more than once, from the sound of it—but he'd never mentioned it to me. I wondered why not.

"Did the cops talk to you . . . Vincent?" I said, trying out the new, improved name. It sounded funny, and Vin laughed when I said it.

"You know what?" he said. "Maybe you should stick to Vin—like always. You know me different from everyone else, Mike. You know everything."

I guess that was why I was there in the first place. We looked at each other for a moment. Boy, it had been a long time, but it didn't feel like it.

Then Vin said, "Yeah, the cops talked to me. They

came to the house. It really scared my mom. She thought they were there for me. They asked me a million questions." He shuddered. "Cops make me nervous, Mike. As soon as they find out about me, they look at me a certain way, you know?"

"I told them that Sal hadn't talked to you in over a year, ever since the thing with Robbie."

"Yeah, well, I guess they thought that after what happened at the convenience store, maybe I had some kind of grudge against Sal. I told them I didn't. How could I be mad at him? But you know what? I'm glad I have an alibi for when it happened—a good one, too. One they can check out and believe. Cops don't like me, Mikey."

I didn't doubt it. I was living with one of those cops.

"What happened, anyway?" he said. "I heard some kids were giving Sal a hard time. My mom said she heard it was probably one of them who did it. It sounded like it was over something dumb."

"You remember Teddy Carlin?"

"Yeah," Vin said. "The guy's a jerk. I ran into him one time after what happened to Robbie." He meant Robbie Ducharme. "You wouldn't believe the stuff he said to me, like he was all of a sudden Robbie's friend, even though I saw him giving Robbie a hard time more than once."

"Teddy likes to give people a hard time," I said.

"He likes to get under people's skin. He sure likes to get under *my* skin," Vin said.

"You remember that girl he used to go with—Staci?"

"Sure." Vin flashed another grin. Staci was the kind of girl he would notice. She was pretty.

"Well, she dumped Teddy, and he's been on her case about it ever since school started. He and those idiots he hangs around with were giving her a hard time. Teddy was mad at Sal, too, because he thought Staci liked Sal. A couple of days ago, I heard him warn Sal to stay away from Staci or else."

"You think Teddy did it?"

"I know there was a lot of shoving going on. And that when he started giving Staci a hard time that day, Sal went to help her. The next thing you know, Sal was—" I couldn't make myself say the word. "He was gone," I said instead. "Can you believe it?"

Vin sighed and leaned back in the booth. "Yeah, well, stuff happens," he said. "I should know."

We looked at each other. I don't know what Vin saw in my eyes, but what I saw in his was that he seemed a lot older than I remembered.

"The cops asked me if he had a weapon," I said.

Vin put down his hamburger, wiped his fingers on a paper napkin, and reached for his milkshake. "What kind of weapon?"

"I don't know. The cop who asked me wouldn't tell me. But he must think that Sal had one, or at least suspect it or have heard something about it, otherwise why would he ask?"

"I can't see Sal with a weapon," Vin said. "Sal is a smart guy, and weapons are stupid."

I couldn't help it. I stared at him.

"You have a knife," I said. "At least, that's what you told me. You said you carried it around sometimes when you were with A. J."

"Well, those days are over. If I get caught with a weapon, you can't believe the trouble I'll be in. Besides, my mom confiscated that knife—not that she had to. I would have handed it over if she'd asked for it."

Boy, he had really changed.

"I don't see Sal with a weapon," he said again.

"So he didn't say anything to you about it?"

"No," Vin said, surprised by the question. "Why would he? We talked a couple of times, Mike. But it had been a long time, and a lot of stuff had happened between us."

"I can't even figure out why he called you up all of a sudden, after everything that happened."

Vin shrugged. "You know Sal," he said. "Maybe he wanted to give me another chance. We used to be tight. Maybe he thought that should mean something. That's the way *I* feel. Real friends can go through a lot of garbage together, right, Mike?"

Sal had gone to see Vin. Despite everything, he had gone to see Vin, more than once. So, yeah, he must have thought that it should mean something. And I did know Sal. So why was I surprised that maybe, just maybe, Sal had looked at everything Vin had done, and somewhere in that mess he had still managed to see the Vin we had grown up with? Boy, if that was true, then it looked like friendship meant more to Sal than it did to me.

"When he came to see me and we were talking, it made me think about all the stuff we did together and how much fun we had. The three of us hanging out, those were the best times I ever had." He shook his head. "I've been wishing lately that I'd done a lot of things differently. Or even just one thing. It's like what they say about butterflies—you know, a butterfly flaps its wings in China and it causes a tornado in America, or something like that. Maybe if I'd done even one thing differently, even something small, it could have changed everything. You know what I mean, Mike?"

I knew exactly what he meant. I stared down at my Coke.

"Hey, Mike?" Vin said. "The number-one thing I found out in the past year—cops aren't as dumb as I always thought they were. Those guys really know what they're doing, especially the Homicide guys. They don't let go. They're going to find out what happened to Sal, you can bet on it."

It was funny to hear those words come out of Vin's mouth after everything he had been through.

» » »

Rebecca was standing outside the church the next day when I got there with Riel and Susan. She came over to us, even though being around Riel usually made her nervous. He had been her history teacher last year, and Rebecca had had trouble separating that from the fact that he was the person I lived with. She still hadn't got over it. She smiled shyly at him, said hello to Susan (who didn't make her nervous at all), and said, "Can I talk to you for a minute, Mike?" Riel and Susan went inside.

"I've been thinking," Rebecca said. "Maybe I shouldn't go on the exchange trip. Maybe I should stay here with you."

Rebecca had been in French immersion all the way from kindergarten to the end of junior high. She was in advanced French now, and her class was going to Quebec City for a week, where they were going to stay with French families. She was supposed to leave Saturday morning. Later in the year, a class of kids from Quebec City was going to come here and stay with the families of the kids in Rebecca's French class.

"You've been looking forward to going," I said, even though I couldn't understand why she would. I would rather have all my teeth drilled than spend a whole week listening to people speak a language I didn't understand very well. "I'll be fine."

"I don't know," she said. "What if something happens?"

I couldn't tell whether she meant what if the cops found out anything or what if I got into more trouble at school.

"If anything happens, I'll let you know," I said. "You should go, Rebecca. Sal would want you to." Sal always wanted good things to happen to people.

Rebecca smiled at me and kissed me on the cheek. Then she looped an arm through mine, and we went into the church together. I spotted Vin up front. He was sitting right behind Sal's parents. In the same pew with him were a couple of other guys, all of them young, but not as young as Vin and me. I guessed that they were Sal's cousins. Riel had told me that they were going to be pallbearers too, and that we should all sit together. So I slid in beside Vin. Rebecca hesitated. She finally sat down next to me.

"You remember Vincent, right, Rebecca?" I said in a quiet voice.

Vin looked appreciatively at Rebecca. She smiled stiffly back at him. Vin leaned close to me so that he could whisper in my ear. "She still doesn't like me, huh?" he said.

"She doesn't really know you," I said.

Rebecca shoved an elbow into my ribs. I decided to stay quiet after that.

The service was really sad, mostly because Sal's mother cried all the way through it. She was sitting right in front of me. Sal's aunt was on one side of her. Sal's dad was on the other side. He stared straight ahead the whole time. If he shed even one tear, I didn't see it. Imogen was in the same pew as Sal's parents. She sniffled all the way through the service. At one time or another, a lot of people were crying. Even me.

At first I thought maybe I shouldn't be crying. After all, it wasn't my first funeral. I'd been to my mother's and then to Billy's. Then I decided that that was exactly what made me cry. It was what made me feel like I couldn't breathe. I knew how bad it felt to lose someone you really cared about. I knew you never got used to them being gone. And I knew it took a long time—a *really* long time—before the hurt turned into a kind of dull pain, like when you were just starting to get a headache. Until it turned into something you could maybe live with.

I glanced at Vin as I rubbed away a tear with the back of my hand. His eyes were dry, but he gave me a sympathetic look. He didn't know anyone close who had died. He didn't feel the same way I did about Sal. And he was different from me. He felt things differently.

When the service was over, the funeral director nodded to Vin and me and the other pallbearers, and we all went up front to walk the casket down the aisle and out of the church. Sal's parents and his aunt and some relatives who had flown in from different countries followed us. I was surprised, as I walked back down the center aisle, to see that Teddy was there. So were Bailey and some of the others. Teddy's eyes met mine as I walked past him, escorting the casket out to a hearse.

When we stepped out of the church, I saw that there were a whole lot of reporters there. Some cameras were following the coffin. Others were taking pictures for the newspaper. After Sal's coffin was loaded into the hearse (I felt sick just looking at it and thinking about it; Sal was in there, and I was never going to see him again), a woman came up to me. She was a reporter. She said, "Excuse me, but I understand you were Salvatore San Miguel's best friend."

"Yeah," I said. I glanced at Vin.

"How do you feel about what happened to your friend?" the reporter said. Some of the other reporters saw her talking to me and crowded in.

"How do I feel?" I said. What kind of stupid question was that? "Someone killed him," I said. "How do you think I feel?"

"There's been a lot of teen violence in the city recently," the woman reporter said. "What do you think is causing that?"

I glanced at Vin again. He just shrugged.

"Look," I said. "All I know is that someone killed Sal, probably someone who goes to my school, and I hope that whoever did it gets what they deserve."

"Someone from your school?" the woman reporter said. "Do you know for sure that it was someone from your school?"

Someone grabbed my elbow. Riel.

"That's enough," he said to the reporter. "He isn't answering any more questions." He pulled me away from the woman, who chased after me and asked again, "Do you know for sure that it was someone from your school?"

Riel pulled me into the church. "Don't talk to them, Mike," he said.

"I was just—"

"I know," he said. "But they're vultures. They ask you questions they have no business asking, and then they print whatever you say. It's better to stay away from them altogether."

I nodded. I hadn't really wanted to talk to that reporter in the first place.

"Now what?" I said.

"There are refreshments in the church hall. We go there."

So that's what we did. As soon as we got to the hall, Rebecca said she was going to help with the food. A moment later a girl came up to me. Her name was Tulla. She worked at McDonald's with Sal. Sometimes, when I went there to grab a pop and see what Sal was up to, I'd find him and Tulla clowning around, joking with each other. I remember Sal telling me that she had a pretty smile, which was why he liked to talk to her. He said she had an even prettier laugh, which was why he liked to joke with her. But she wasn't laughing or smiling now. There were tears in her eyes.

"Hey, Mike," she said. "It's hard to believe, huh?"

Yeah.

"He was such a good guy. He was always helping people. He really went the distance, you know?"

I told her I sure did.

"I can't believe anyone would kill him," she said.

But someone had.

"The store manager came." She pointed him out to me. He was talking to Sal's parents. When I said that it was nice of him to show up, she said, "It would be even nicer if he called Sal by his right name. He was always calling him Sam. Sal corrected him for a while, then I think he just gave up. I hope he doesn't call him Sam when he's talking to Sal's parents."

"Well, it's still nice that he came," I said. I couldn't imagine Mr. Geordi showing up for my funeral.

"Maybe. But the guy's a dork," Tulla said. "Sal told me that when Mr. Torrence took over, working conditions got bad fast. Almost everyone who worked there was gone within two months. Sal was the only person working there who had been there before the summer. Everyone else is brand new. And you still wouldn't believe the turnover. I only stayed because Sal was so much fun. He was the best shift manager ever."

Vin came over to me a few minutes later, nudged me, and nodded across the room to where Rebecca was walking around with a plate of little sandwiches.

"She's really your girlfriend, huh?" he said. "Way to go, Mike."

But I didn't say anything because just then Teddy and Bailey and the rest of them came into the hall and headed for the food. I couldn't believe it. All of the people in the hall—except Teddy and his gang—were friends of Sal's or friends of his family's. Or they were kids who went to my school who liked Sal. Or teachers who had known Sal and who respected him. Or people who had worked with him.

Teddy and his friends were the ones who had given Sal a hard time because he'd tried to help Staci. But there they were, standing all together now, holding little plates of sandwiches and talking to each other. At least they were quiet for a change. Sara D. was pressed up against Teddy. A girl named Annie was holding Bailey's hand. The rest of the guys—Steven and Matt and them—all stuck together.

While I was looking at them, Miranda walked over to Teddy. She said something to him. I couldn't believe it. She must have heard what had happened by now. Why was she even going near him? Why did she smile at him like that?

Teddy looked across the room, right at me. He gave me a little nod. That did it. I started toward him.

"Whoa," Vin said. He grabbed my arm. "Where are you going?"

"Let me go," I said.

But Vin held tight. He looked from me to Teddy and back to me again. Teddy gave him a little nod, too. What was that all about? What was he doing here? Why did he even think he had a right to be here after what he had done?

"I know how you feel," Vin said quietly. "Like I said, the guy's a jerk. But take a look around, Mike. You don't want to do anything stupid in front of Sal's parents, do you?"

Teddy took a pack of cigarettes out of his pocket and headed for the closest exit. Sara D., the girl who was trying hard to be Staci's replacement, went with him. The rest of them stayed behind.

I headed for the same door Teddy had just gone through.

"Hey," Vin said. He caught up to me and followed

me outside.

We found Teddy and Sara D. out in the parking lot behind the church. Teddy was lighting a cigarette. I headed straight over to him.

"You have no right being here," I said.

Teddy looked at me and opened his mouth to say something. But then Vin stepped up and said, "Is this how you get your kicks these days, Teddy? You crash funerals?"

Teddy took a puff of his cigarette and smiled at Vin. "I heard they let you out," he said. "I also heard they won't let you come back to our school. Guess they don't want any more kids to be kicked to death, huh?"

Vin was right about Teddy. He liked to get under people's skin. He was doing it now.

Vin's eyes hardened. Even though he'd been there when Robbie was kicked, he had always denied he was involved. But he'd been arrested anyway and was convicted of aggravated assault and had even done some time in a juvenile facility. He stepped in closer to Teddy. Sara D. stuck close to Teddy, maybe to show him that she didn't scare easily. Maybe she thought he'd respect her for that, but, if you ask me, Teddy didn't even notice. He was watching Vin. He didn't want any nasty surprises.

"Sal was a friend of mine," Vin said.

Teddy laughed when he heard that. "Yeah," he said. "He was such a good friend that he turned you in to the cops. I bet you're *real* sorry about what happened to him."

Everything happened fast after that.

Vin's foot flew out and caught Teddy right in the stomach. Teddy hurtled backward and then down and landed on the pavement with a loud *oomph!* Vin started toward him. I tried to catch him, but I was too slow. Sara D. ran back into the church. For sure that was going to mean trouble.

"We'd better go back inside," I said to Vin.

I couldn't tell if he heard me. He reached down and grabbed Teddy by the lapels of his jacket and jerked him to his feet. That's when I noticed for the first time just how much Vin had changed. He'd gotten taller, sure, but he'd also gotten a whole lot stronger. He was shaking Teddy like he was a rag doll. Teddy grabbed both of Vin's arms and tried to pull free. Right then, Vin released him, and Teddy landed butt-first on the pavement again.

"Come on," Vin said to him. "You want more?"

Teddy sat on the ground, looking up at Vin for a moment. Then—I'd never seen anyone move so fast— he sprang up and launched himself headfirst at Vin, tackling him and taking him down for a hard landing on the pavement. I heard something crack. I sure hoped it wasn't Vin's head. Teddy got on top of Vin and started to hammer at him with both fists—at least, that's what he was trying to do. Vin was fighting back as best he could. Teddy pinned one of Vin's arms under his knee and started to work on pinning down the other one.

I grabbed Teddy from behind and started to drag him off Vin. That gave Vin the opening he needed to buck free of Teddy. I had both of Teddy's arms wrenched around behind his back, and Vin was getting ready to swing at him, when a hand landed on my shoulder. I figured it must be one of Teddy's friends, so I whirled around with my fists up.

It was Riel. He did not look pleased.

He pushed me away from Teddy and then turned on Vin, who was smart enough to back away without being told. Riel examined Teddy.

"You okay?" he said.

Teddy just shrugged. Sara D. ran up to him and put her arm around his waist and asked him if he was hurt. Within a couple of seconds, the rest of Teddy's friends were crowded around him. I felt myself tense up. There were eight or nine of them, and I started to imagine what would have happened if they had showed up before Riel.

"You want to press charges?" Riel said to Teddy.

I stared at him. Whose side was he on?

Teddy laughed at the question. "So what if I do?" he said. "You're a cop. You expect me to believe you'd play it straight, you'd let your own kid go down for assaulting me?"

"If that's what happened," Riel said.

Teddy shook his head. "Right," he said.

He turned and walked away. Sara D. was still holding onto him like she thought maybe he'd fall down if she didn't. Bailey took a long, hard look at me before he turned away, too. Annie slipped her hand into his, but he pulled away from her. The rest of them fell into step behind Bailey.

Riel turned to me. "What were you thinking?" he

said. "You already hit that boy once and nearly broke his nose."

That surprised me. I hadn't told him what had happened at school, but obviously Mr. Gianneris had. But Riel hadn't mentioned it. Maybe he'd decided to do what Mr. Gianneris had done—give me a break. Until now.

"It was my fault," Vin said.

Riel looked him over with obvious distaste. He didn't like Vin. He had never liked him.

"Teddy said something that made me mad, and I hit him," Vin said. "He got me pinned down. Mike was just trying to get him off me. The whole thing was my fault."

Riel looked at him for another few moments, his eyes sharp, his mouth a thin, angry line, clamped shut maybe so that he wouldn't say something he might regret.

"I was looking for you," Riel said to me. "Sal's father isn't feeling well, so I'm going to take him home and stay with him until someone else can get home. I think you'd better come with me." He turned and looked pointedly at Vin.

"I guess I should take off," Vin said. "See you around, Mike."

"Yeah. See you."

"I'm going inside to get Sal's father," Riel said. "Meet me at the car. You got it, Mike?"

"You heard what Vin said, right?" I said. "I was just trying—"

"Go," Riel said.

Jeez.

I stalked past him toward the church parking lot. Vin fell into step beside me. He had to know Riel wouldn't like that. I sure did. But he did it anyway, and I didn't try to stop him.

"We could just take off," I said to him when we were out of earshot of Riel.

"He told you to wait for him, Mike," Vin said.

"We could go downtown, maybe shoot some pool."

"Come on, Mike. If you do something like that, you're going to piss off Riel. You don't want to do that."

"Says who?"

Vin shook his head. "You've got a nice place to live. I heard you're doing okay in school."

"Who told you that?"

"Sal."

"You and Sal talked about *me*?"

"We used to be friends," Vin said. "All three of us. I wanted to know how you were doing, so I asked and, yeah, we talked about you."

"If you wanted to know how I was doing, you could have asked me."

"I guess. But you were pretty mad at me the last time I saw you. Besides, I didn't want to call your place. What if Riel answered? He doesn't like me, and you know it. But he's a good guy, Mike. Since you've been living with him, you've been doing okay. You've got a nice girl-friend. So far the biggest trouble you've been in is strictly small-time. You don't want to mess that up, do you?"

Truthfully, the way I was feeling, I didn't care.

"Sal wouldn't want you to mess it up," Vin said. "Not even on his account. So do yourself a favor. Wait at the car like Riel told you."

"Someone killed him, Vin."

"I know."

"What if it was Teddy? Isn't that why you hit him?"

"I hit him because he made it sound like Sal wasn't my friend, like I should be glad he's dead. But Teddy, stick someone with a knife?" He shook his head. "I don't know. If it was Teddy, the cops will figure it out. Come on, Mike. Do the right thing."

"Like you just did?" I said.

"Yeah, well, nobody's perfect, huh?"

CHAPTER EIGHT

Riel came out of the church again a few minutes later and started in with a lecture: What had gotten into me? Why was I going out of my way to get into trouble? He understood how I felt—he really did—it was terrible what had happened to Sal, he was such a good kid, he always worked hard, he never gave anyone a hard time, he was a real role model, the kind of person I should aspire to be.

"I'm not saying you're a bad kid, Mike. You're not. But it's times like these that really show a person's character. A man who can handle himself well when things are bad is a man who can always handle himself. You hear what I'm saying, Mike?"

Yeah, I heard. But: "Vin told you the truth. I didn't start it."

"Maybe," Riel said. What did he mean: *Maybe?* Was he doubting me? "But from where I was standing, it looked like you were planning to finish it. What were you even doing with Vin, anyway?"

"He's my friend," I said.

"I thought that was over. I thought you two had gone

your separate ways."

I could have tried to explain it to him: Sal and I went back a long way. But Vin and I went back even further. We had played trucks in the sandbox together. We'd horsed around together. I had known Vin ten times longer than I had known Riel. I had known both of them longer than I had known Riel. And now Sal was gone, and if I felt like being with Vin, that was nobody's business but mine. So what if he had messed up? He was trying to get back on track. He was going to school. He was on probation. He knew if he messed up again, he'd be in big trouble, so he wasn't doing anything that he wasn't supposed to be doing—well, except maybe when someone like Teddy got under his skin. But so what? Teddy got what he deserved. The main thing about Vin was that I could talk to him without always having to explain myself.

I could have tried to tell Riel that. But I didn't think he would get it. All he saw when he looked at Vin was a guy who had done a lot of really stupid stuff and had even gotten himself locked up for it. Riel was a cop. To him, Vin was a criminal. So what was the point of talking about it? I'd only be wasting my breath.

"Well?" Riel said.

"Well what? I thought we were taking Sal's dad home."

Riel stared at me for a moment. "We are," he said.

"How come you have to stay with him?"

"His only child was just murdered, Mike. He's already sick, and this could make things worse. Sal's mom is worried about him. She's afraid to leave him alone right now."

I was going to ask what she was afraid of. But then I got it. I felt sorry for Sal's mom. If there was some way things could have been worse for her, I sure didn't see it.

Sal's aunt came out of the church with Sal's dad, and together they walked over to Riel's car. Sal's dad didn't look at either Riel or me. He seemed to be in a different world. His face was blank, his skin was pale, and the suit he was wearing hung on him like it was a couple of sizes too big. Riel opened the front passenger door for him, and he got in without saying a word. Sal's aunt said that she appreciated what Riel was doing. She said that she and Maria—Sal's mom—would get home as soon as they could, but so many people had turned up at the funeral and Maria didn't want to leave before everyone else did. Riel told her it was no problem. He said they should take as much time as they needed and that they shouldn't worry about it. Then he nodded at me and we got into the car.

Sal's father didn't say a single word the whole way home, and Riel didn't push him. He pulled up in front of the building where Sal's parents lived, and we all got out of the car again. Sal's father took out some keys and unlocked the main door. He climbed silently up to the top floor of the three-story building and walked down the hall to the back. But he didn't open the door. He just stood there with the keys in his hands. Then, just like that, he started to sob.

Riel said something to him in quiet Spanish. He took the keys from Sal's dad, handed them to me, and nodded at the door. I had to try three different keys before I found the one that unlocked the apartment. As soon as I opened the door, I knew something was wrong.

The living room had been trashed. All the cushions were off the sofas. There were magazines and newspapers everywhere. Sal's aunt had a desk in one corner of the dining room. All the drawers were open, and it looked like every scrap of paper in them had been thrown onto the floor. Riel took one look at the mess and pulled his cell phone out of his pocket. Sal's father went into the apartment and looked around like he couldn't believe what he was seeing. His face was wet from crying, but his eyes were wide now as he saw what had happened.

"Bring Sal's dad back out here into the hall," Riel said. "Don't let him touch anything." Then he started talking into his phone. He was talking to the cops.

I stepped inside to get Sal's dad, like Riel had said. But he wasn't in the living room anymore. He had gone down the hallway that led to the bedrooms. I found him in Sal's room, which looked like a tornado had ripped through it. There was paper everywhere. The drawers to his dresser and his desk had been ripped out, everything in them dumped out onto the floor, and the drawers thrown against the wall. His pillows had been slashed. So had his mattress. His desk lamp had been broken. There was a little book—an address book—lying open on the floor. It looked like most of the pages had been ripped out. Maybe Sal had done that. Maybe someone else had. But Sal's father didn't seem to notice any of that. He was kneeling down in the middle of Sal's room, and he was picking up a picture. There was broken glass on the floor from a couple of broken picture frames, and Sal's dad must have cut his hand on a piece of it because I saw blood on his hand. He picked up the picture—both pieces of it.

"Mr. San Miguel," I said. "We should go back outside. John is calling the police."

Sal's dad kept staring at the picture. I reached out and pulled it gently out of his hands. It was a picture of Sal in his McDonald's uniform. He was with a bunch of his co-workers. The ones on either side of him—both women—had their arms around him, and almost everyone in the picture was smiling. Someone had ripped the picture in half diagonally. No wonder his father was so upset.

"We have to leave things the way they are," I said. I put the two halves of the picture back onto the floor and tugged on Sal's dad's arm, but he wouldn't move. He bent down again and picked up the picture. Then Riel appeared.

"Mike, I told you—" he said. Then he stopped. He glanced at the torn picture Sal's dad was holding. He said something in Spanish to Sal's dad. He didn't try to take the picture out of his hands. He put his hand on Sal's dad's shoulder and guided him out of the room and out of the apartment.

"Take him down to the car and stay with him," Riel said. He handed me his keys.

"What about that picture?" I said.

"If whoever did this was wearing gloves, it doesn't matter. If they weren't—" He looked around. "—there'll be other prints. Let him keep the picture for now."

I led Sal's dad downstairs and unlocked the car. He got in the front passenger seat. I got in behind the wheel.

"I'm really sorry this happened," I said. I knew it wouldn't do any good, but I felt I had to say something.

A few minutes later, a police car turned up and two uniformed cops went inside. They were in there for a while. Then a taxi pulled up, and Susan and Sal's mom got out. They came over to the car, and I got out.

"John's inside," I said.

"I know," Susan said. "He called me and asked me to bring Maria home. He wants her to check if anything valuable is missing."

Sal's mother opened the passenger door and said something to Sal's dad. He didn't answer. She closed the door again and went into the apartment building. She was in there a long time. While she was gone, a Forensic Ident truck drove up and some more cops went inside. It seemed like forever before Riel and Sal's mom came out again. Riel opened one of the rear doors, and Sal's mom got in. I climbed out from behind the steering wheel.

"We're taking Sal's parents to our place for a while," Riel said to me.

"Why would anyone break into Sal's apartment?" I said. I was so angry that I was shaking. "Do you think it was the person who killed Sal?" But no, as soon as I said that, I knew I was wrong. Teddy and the rest of them had been at the funeral. They'd been there the whole time.

"It's possible," Riel said. "I put in a call to Dave. Or maybe it was someone who saw the notice in the newspaper. It happens sometimes—someone sees a death notice in the paper. They see when the funeral is going to be and they figure that no one will be home—it's the perfect time for a break-in."

"Did they take a lot of stuff?"

"Some jewelry. Approximately one hundred dollars in cash. Sal's computer."

"His laptop?" I said. Sal had bought it secondhand. It only cost him a couple of hundred dollars, but, still, he had put in a lot of hours over the summer so he could afford it.

Riel nodded grimly.

"Thieves like that, they're worse than vultures. They prey on people when they're at their most vulnerable. If you ask me, that makes them the lowest of the low. Get in the car, Mike."

I climbed in back beside Susan.

The drive from Sal's aunt's apartment to Riel's house didn't take long, but it felt like forever. The only person who said anything was Riel, and it was all in Spanish. I think he was explaining to Sal's parents what the police were doing because the only word I recognized was *policia*, and he said it a couple of times. When we finally got to the house, Sal's mom had to touch Sal's dad's arm before he realized that the car had stopped. He was still holding the ripped picture. He'd been staring at it all the way to the house.

We all went inside, and Susan made tea for everyone. I didn't know what to say, but Susan and Riel managed to keep a conversation going with Sal's mom. She started to cry a couple of times, but that didn't seem to make them uncomfortable. Susan got a box of tissues from the kitchen and put it on the table near Sal's mom. I guess they figured crying was normal under the circumstances, and I guess they were right.

Eventually the phone rang and Riel answered it. When he finished the call, he said, "I can take you home now if you'd like." Sal's mom hugged Susan. On the way out, Sal's dad handed me the ripped photograph. I didn't know if he wanted me to look at it or say something about it or what. But it turned out he was giving it to me. Maybe it was too hard for him to look at. Maybe he didn't want it anymore because it was ruined, so maybe he wanted me to throw it out. I looked at it. Sal was smiling out at the camera. When I went upstairs to go get changed for work, I took the picture with me and put it in the top drawer of my desk. Maybe it was ripped, but it was still Sal, and I didn't have any recent pictures of him.

>> >> >>

The next morning when I got up, Riel was waiting for me in the kitchen. He handed me the newspaper, which was open to a page with a picture of—guess who?—me on it. The caption underneath the picture said my name and that I was the best friend of Toronto's "latest victim of youth crime." The article that went with the picture quoted me as saying that the killer probably went to my school.

"That's why you have to be careful about talking to reporters," Riel said. "Something like that just gets people all worked up."

"I said *probably*," I said. "But I bet I'm right. I bet it *is* someone from my school. I bet it's Teddy."

"Just steer clear of reporters, Mike," Riel said. "When we know something for sure, *we'll* talk to them."

"When *we* know something?" I said, and, yeah, I guess it came off sounding sarcastic, because Riel gave me a sharp look.

"It's not my case, Mike," Riel said. "It's not even my area anymore."

Right.

» » »

Going to school after the funeral was even worse than going to school the day after Sal had died. That day, people had been in shock. People had been crying. People had been talking about Sal. They'd said nice things about him. But when I walked into school on Tuesday morning, after the funeral, everything was back to normal. Nobody was talking about Sal. Nobody was crying over him. It was like he had never existed. And then an announcement came over the PA system: we were going to have a special assembly. What made it special was that the cops were there—a couple of uniforms and two plainclothes guys. One of them was Dave Jones. Ms. Rather, the principal, introduced him and told us that we should pay close attention to what he was going to say. She said it was a terrible thing to lose a student and a member of our school community—that's what she called it, a community—and that everyone should do everything they could to cooperate with the police so that they could find whoever had done this awful thing.

Then Dave Jones stepped up to the microphone. For a couple of minutes he didn't say a word. He just looked out at all of the faces that were looking back at him. Maybe he was clocking us, checking out who met his gaze and who turned away or bowed their head. Maybe not. Finally he said, "You all know what happened last Thursday at lunchtime. You all know that at approximately 12:30 p.m., Salvatore San Miguel was stabbed in the chest and that he died of his wounds. The incident happened approximately half a block east of the school. I know that many of you were out on the street when it happened. I know that some of you saw Sal. That's why I'm here today—to ask for your help."

He paused and scanned the auditorium again. He looked right at me, but only for a split second.

"Sal was sixteen years old," he said. "He was on the honor roll last year despite the fact that he held down a job to help support his family. The people I've talked to who knew Sal all liked him. They say that he was a reliable, responsible person, that he had a good sense of humor, that he was nice to everyone, and that he helped out whenever he could. His parents are devastated by his death, as I imagine any of your parents would be if it had been you. A lot of you knew Sal. You were in classes with him. You saw him around school—maybe in the cafeteria or the library or just in passing in the halls. Maybe you ate at the McDonald's where he worked."

He paused and looked around again. "I've talked to many of you personally," he said. "But I'm asking again—if anyone in this room saw anything—and I mean *anything*—out on the street the day that Sal was killed, even if you're not sure it's important, I'm asking you to talk to me. If you know anything or have heard anything, talk to me. Or, if you don't feel comfortable doing that, I'm asking you to call the TIPS line." He told us the phone number, and Ms. Rather put it up on an overhead screen behind him. "You don't have to give your name if you don't want to. And there's no call display on the phones there. We won't know who's calling. It's one hundred percent anonymous. So I'm asking you, if you know anything or saw anything, let us know. Help us find the person who killed Sal San Miguel. Please."

He stepped back then, and Ms. Rather repeated the phone number and the fact that calls could be made anonymously. She said, "Imagine if this happened to your brother or your sister. Imagine if this happened to your best friend. If you knew something, you'd tell. Sal didn't have any brothers or sisters. But he has parents who love him very much. And I know he had friends. Good friends. I know that some of them are right here in this room. And I hope that if any of you know or saw anything, you'll do the right thing."

I heard someone sobbing softly to my right. When I turned my head, I saw that it was Kim. But you know what? I didn't care.

>> >> >>

I had math after the assembly, but I didn't even bother to open my book. By lunchtime I thought I would go crazy. I went to Rebecca's locker to find her, but when I got there, all of a sudden I couldn't breathe. I had to get outside and get some air. I turned and ran for the stairs just as Rebecca rounded the corner and spotted me.

"Mike?" Rebecca called. "Where are you going?"

People turned to look at me—and all I could do was wonder if any of them had been out on the street last Thursday, if any of them had turned and looked at Sal the way they were looking at me now, looking, but not doing anything. It was a good thing Mr. Gianneris wasn't around. If he'd seen the way I raced down those stairs, shoving people out of my way, he'd have handed me a detention for sure. I walked and walked and walked until I knew there was no way I was going to make it back to school on time for my next period.

Sure enough, I was twenty minutes late and got tagged

by the hall monitor. It didn't matter. I couldn't concentrate. I might as well have skipped the afternoon, too.

» » »

Rebecca was waiting at my locker after school.

"Are you okay, Mike?" she said.

"I'm fine."

"Are you sure? Because you heard that announcement on Friday, right, Mike? The one that said if anyone was having trouble, you know, with what happened, with dealing with it, they could talk to someone about it. About what they're feeling, I mean."

"I'm fine, Rebecca."

She watched me open my locker.

"When they made that announcement, I thought about you, Mike." She slipped her backpack off her shoulder and rooted around in it for a few moments before she found her school agenda. She opened it and handed me a slip of paper with her neat printing on it.

"What's this?"

"I wrote down the name and phone number of the counselor they mentioned. I thought maybe you might want to—"

"You thought I might want to what? Talk to a shrink?"

"It's a counselor, not a shrink," Rebecca said. "It's someone people can talk to about what they're feeling and about what grieving is."

"I'm *okay*, Rebecca," I said. But I was starting to feel all tight inside.

"You've been acting different, Mike."

"Different? Jeez, my best friend just died. Doesn't everyone act different when something like that happens?"

"Well, sure," she said. But something was bothering her. I could tell by the little lines between her eyes and by the way she kept looking at me.

"What?" I said. I was trying not to get irritated, mainly because I like Rebecca. If it had been anyone else, I'm not sure what I would have said or done.

"Don't get mad, Mike," she said.

"Mad? About what?"

"Promise?"

I had no idea what she was talking about. "Okay, I promise," I said. The tight feeling inside me got tighter.

"It's just that you attacked Teddy on Friday and again at the funeral," Rebecca said slowly. I wondered who had told her what had happened at the funeral. I sure hadn't. "And you made Kim cry."

"*What?* When did I do that?"

"On Thursday, after she told you what she told the police. She thinks you blame her for what happened to Sal."

"That's not what I said."

"Well, it sounded like that was what you were saying. I was there, Mike. I heard you. You more or less said that Kim should have done something when Teddy and them started in on Staci. But she's just one person, Mike."

"So what if that's what I said?" Why was she sticking

up for Kim anyway? "It's true, isn't it? Are you telling me you want me to apologize to her even though she was right there but she didn't do anything to help him?"

"You know what I think?" Rebecca said. "I think you got mad at Kim because of your history book."

"*What?*"

"You lost your history book, so you had to borrow mine. Then you forgot mine at home when I needed it."

"I gave it back to you on Friday, Rebecca."

"I know. But that's not what I'm saying."

"What *are* you saying?"

"You forgot my book at home, so you had to bail on your plans to go downtown with Sal so he could take the test for his driver's license." She laid a hand on my arm. "If you hadn't lost your history book or if you hadn't forgotten mine at home, you and Sal would have been downtown. He wouldn't have been anywhere near Teddy and the rest of them. He wouldn't have gone to help Staci—he wouldn't even have known that anyone was hassling her."

I stared at her. She wasn't saying anything I hadn't been thinking ever since it had happened, and she didn't even know the whole story. But it's one thing to think something privately in your own head and a whole other thing to find out that someone else was thinking the same thing, that someone else was doing the same thing I was doing—holding me responsible. I don't know why—well, maybe I do—but it made me mad.

"Are you're saying it was *my* fault, Rebecca?"

"No. I'm just saying . . ." She hesitated, like she was searching for the right words. "I'm just saying that I understand how you feel. I mean, you're probably thinking that if you hadn't forgotten my book at home, things would have been different. And maybe that's why you're so mad at everyone."

"I'm mad at everyone because nobody did anything to help Sal," I said. "And because probably someone who goes to our school—or maybe even a whole bunch of kids who go to our school—killed him, and so far nothing is happening."

"I understand," Rebecca said. "Which is why I think it would be a good idea for you to talk to someone. It could really help."

I had to bite my tongue. I like Rebecca. I like her more than I've ever liked any girl. Maybe I even like her more than I've ever liked anyone, period. But she was driving me crazy. I didn't want to talk to anyone. I just wanted the cops to find out who had killed Sal. I wanted them to arrest that person and put him in prison for the rest of his life—except that if it was a kid, if it was Teddy, for example, that wasn't going to happen. No way he'd get that long. He'd be out in a couple of years—assuming the cops got their act together and caught him in the first place. But Sal would stay dead forever.

It wasn't fair. None of it was.

Then . . . wait a minute.

"How did you know that I was planning to go downtown with Sal?" I said. "I don't remember telling you."

"You didn't," Rebecca said. I saw a flash of something in her eyes—like she was mad I hadn't told her. "Imogen mentioned it."

"Imogen? You talked to *Imogen*?" The only good thing about Imogen was that she had transferred schools this year, so I didn't have to see her face every day.

"I called her after it happened," Rebecca said. "And I talked to her at the funeral."

"You *called* her? What for?"

Rebecca took her hand off my arm and looked closely at me.

"Didn't Sal tell you about Imogen?" she said.

I started jamming stuff into my locker, mainly so I wouldn't have to look at Rebecca.

"Tell me what?" I said.

"Imogen said he was going to tell you." She touched my arm again and gave it a little tug so that there was nothing else I could do—I had to look at her. "Sal was going out with her again, Mike."

I looked at her and said, "What are you talking about? Imogen tried to get me arrested. She spread all kinds of rumors about me. She accused me of beating up Sal. She practically accused me of—" I shook my head. "I can't believe you called her."

Rebecca stood up straighter now. Her cheeks turned pink.

"She was going out with Sal," she said. "They'd been seeing each other since the summer, and Sal was trying to get up his courage to tell you."

"His *courage?* Now you're saying Sal was afraid to talk to me?"

"Well, I guess he knew how you'd react ..."

"I can't believe you called her, Rebecca."

Rebecca drew in a deep breath. I could see she was working hard at staying calm. "I knew she still liked him, Mike. I knew she was upset when they broke up. So I called her to see how she was doing. And I don't need you to yell at me about it."

"I wasn't yelling."

"Yes, you were. You're mad at me, and I don't know why. I didn't do anything wrong."

"Oh, and *I* did, is that it? If I hadn't lost my history book and hadn't borrowed yours and then forgotten it at home, Sal would still be alive? Isn't that what you said?"

"That's not what I meant," she said.

"But it's what you said. You think this is all my fault."

"No, I don't," she said. She seemed stunned by the suggestion.

I slammed my locker door. The *bang* reverberated up and down the hall. A lot of people turned to look.

Rebecca stared at me for a moment. Her lower lip was trembling, and her eyes got all watery. But she didn't cry. Instead, she pulled herself up straight and slung her backpack over her shoulder. She didn't say a word as she turned and marched down the hall.

Jeez, what was I doing?

I jammed my lock through the loop in my locker door and chased after her.

"Rebecca, wait," I said.

But she was already halfway down the stairs.

"Hey, Rebecca!"

I ran after her—and collided with Mr. Gianneris.

Terrific. I waited, but he didn't get mad at me the way he usually did when he caught me breaking some stupid rule—like, no running on the stairs. Instead he said, "Slow it down, huh, Mike?" and let it go at that.

By the time I got outside, Rebecca was gone.

» » »

I started to walk over to Rebecca's house but ended up taking a detour. Actually, I took two. First, I crossed the street and stood at the opening to the alley where they had found Sal. I stood there for a long time, feeling all shaky inside, before I finally made myself step into the alley. It ran straight for a couple of meters, then it made a sharp turn and ran behind the backs of stores and restaurants until it finally hit another main street. It also connected to other alleys. Kids cut through there all the time, some because it was a shortcut to get where they were going, others because it was somewhere to hang out where, mostly, people couldn't see what you were doing.

I turned to leave. That's when I noticed the big dark spot on the grey dust and gravel. At least, that's what I thought it was at first. I was turning, I looked down, and I thought, *dark spot*. It took a moment until I realized what had made that spot so dark. Blood. Sal's blood. I felt sick inside. I turned and ran out of the alley. I stood on the sidewalk, sweating and feeling like I was going to throw up. Then I decided to take a short walk so that I could calm down before I tried to talk to Rebecca.

I ended up a dozen blocks north of school, in the ravine that snaked for maybe five kilometers between a whole bunch of high-rise apartment buildings. It was nice and quiet in there. A person could think in there.

And that's exactly what I did.

I thought.

The main thing I thought about was why Dave Jones had asked me if Sal had a weapon. Why would a guy like Sal have a weapon? Why would he even need one? But that's what Dave had asked. He'd also asked me if Sal was being bullied. Had something been going on that I didn't know about? *Had* someone being bullying Sal? Had it been so bad that Sal thought he needed some kind of weapon to protect himself?

Boy, and that opened the floodgates. Those two questions led to a dozen more, like:

Suppose that was true? Suppose Teddy had done more than just jab Sal a couple of times. Suppose he had threatened him in a way that really scared Sal? If he had, why hadn't Sal told me? We were supposed to have been friends. But he'd gone back with Imogen, and the way Rebecca had put it, he'd been afraid to tell me. Was there other stuff he was afraid to tell me or didn't want to tell me or didn't trust me with? And if there was, what did *that* mean? I thought he was my best friend. Had that changed without me even noticing? Was it because of what I did after that convenience store robbery? But Vin had been way more involved than me, so if that was it, why had he started getting friendly with Vin again?

Then I thought, *Listen to yourself, Mike. Sal is dead, and here you are feeling sorry for yourself because maybe Sal didn't see you as his friend anymore, as if that even matters now. As if it's important.*

It wasn't.

The only thing that was important was who had killed him.

Thinking about that made me wonder about a lot of things, like:

First, why had Sal gone into that alley? Had he been steering Staci in there, maybe to get her away from Teddy? If he had been, why hadn't Staci seen what happened? Or had she? If she had, had she told the cops? No, that didn't make sense. If Staci had seen what had happened and if she had told the cops, then the cops wouldn't have come to school today to ask for everyone's help. So that must mean she hadn't seen anything. Either that, or she hadn't told the cops what she saw. If she knew something that she wasn't telling, what did that mean?

Second, if Sal was stabbed in that alley, then someone else was in there with him. Had that person gone into the alley after Sal? Was it Teddy? Was it one of Teddy's gang? Was it a couple of them? If it was, someone must have seen them go in there—someone who so far hadn't said anything to the police.

Or was it someone else, someone who was maybe waiting for Sal in the alley? I shook my head. That didn't make sense. How could anyone possibly know that Sal was going to go into that particular alley on that particular day at that particular time? After all, Sal wasn't even supposed to be there. He was supposed to be downtown, writing his driver's license test. So it had to be someone who followed him into the alley. Followed him, killed him, and then got away.

One thing was certain. Whether or not anyone had said anything to the cops, six days later, the cops still didn't have a solid lead on who killed Sal. That was why Dave Jones had come to school and practically begged kids to come forward and say what they knew. The cops didn't have a clue. That's why they were asking dumb questions—like, did Sal have a weapon?

I sat down on a rock that was set way back on the path. There was no one around. I put my head down on my knees, and just like that, I was crying.

Jeez.

CHAPTER NINE

Both Susan and Riel came into the front hall when I finally got home. Susan looked worried and relieved both at the same time. Riel looked worried and annoyed.

"Where have you been?" he said. "It's been dark for over an hour. You missed supper. You didn't call."

"I took a walk," I said.

"Taking a walk is one thing," Riel said. "Worrying us sick is another."

Susan touched his arm, and he stopped talking.

"Have you had anything to eat, Mike?" she said.

I shook my head.

"Are you hungry?"

"I guess."

"Come into the kitchen," she said. "I'll get you some supper."

I followed her inside. Riel came too. He sat across the table from me while Susan took down a plate and opened the fridge.

"Rebecca called," he said. When I didn't say anything, he said, "Is everything okay between you two?"

"Yeah," I said. "I guess. I don't know."

"At a time like this, it's easy for everything to go off the rails, Mike," Riel said. "Believe me, I know."

I wanted to tell him he didn't know, that his best friend hadn't just been killed. Except that that wasn't exactly true. One of Riel's partners had been shot right in front of him. Riel had been shot, too, but he had survived. He'd stopped being a cop for a while after that. So I guess he had a pretty good idea what it felt like.

Susan slid a plate in front of me—lasagna and garlic bread. She put a glass of milk on the table, too.

"There's seconds if you want," she said.

I thanked her. She left Riel and me alone in the kitchen.

I poked at the lasagna.

"Are you sure you're okay, Mike?" Riel said.

"How come Teddy is still walking around? How come he hasn't been arrested?"

"I don't know."

I looked at him. If you didn't know him, you'd think he was telling the truth. But that would be because if you didn't know him, you wouldn't know he'd been a cop for most of his adult life. You wouldn't know that Dave Jones was his friend. You wouldn't know that cops talked about things with each other that they didn't talk about with other people.

"But he's a suspect, right?"

"I don't know, Mike."

"He threatened Sal."

"You have to be patient, Mike. If Teddy did it, Dave

will find out. He'll make the case."

If Teddy did it.

"Eat your supper, Mike."

I shoved a forkful of lasagna into my mouth. Boy, Susan sure could cook. That one bite made me realize how long it had been since the doughnut that was all I'd eaten for lunch. I took another bite, then another.

» » »

That night, I dreamed about Teddy. I dreamed he was laughing at me. I dreamed he got away with murder.

Rebecca came to the house first thing the next morning, which surprised me, considering how I had treated her the last time I'd seen her. We went outside where we could talk in private. We faced each other, and at exactly the same time we both said, "I'm sorry."

"I shouldn't have yelled at you," I said.

"I should have been more sensitive to your feelings," she said.

"But you were right," I said. "I *have* been acting like a jerk."

"I never said—"

"You didn't have to, Rebecca. I'm sorry I made Kim cry. I was just so mad."

"I know."

"But I'm not sorry I hit Teddy."

"I know, Mike." She looped one arm through mine, and we walked to school together.

I kept my head down all day. I didn't want to look at anyone or talk to anyone except Rebecca. After school, I had to go to work.

I had only been at work for about half an hour when I looked up and saw Staci coming down the aisle where I was shelving a dozen different kinds of pickles. Alex was at the other end of the aisle, restocking instant soups and noodles. Staci had one of those little baskets people use when they're only buying a few things, not doing a whole week's shopping, and she was carrying what looked like a shopping list. She stopped in front of the display of cooking sauces—curry sauces and sauces in a jar that you pour over meat while it's cooking. She stood there for a couple of minutes, studying all the jars. Finally she shook her head, which is how I knew she was having trouble finding what she was looking for.

"Can I help you?" I said. I saw Alex at the other end of the aisle turn in my direction. He must have thought I was talking to him. Well, why not? He had already messed up a few times this shift—he'd dropped a couple of glass jars of expensive soup and then, when he went to get the mop to clean up the mess he'd made, he had accidentally knocked a couple of cartons of eggs off the shelf. Both times I had helped him. The reason Mr. Geordi had given him instant soups and noodles to restock now was that if you dropped the packages, they didn't break.

Staci looked over at me. "I'm supposed to get some tomato sauce, but I don't see it."

"Tomato sauce is in aisle five," I said, "next to the pasta."

"Thanks," she said. She hesitated. "You and Sal were close, weren't you?"

I nodded.

"He was nice," she said. "It's funny. We went to the same school for a couple of years, but I only got to know him this year."

I didn't see what was so funny about that. You don't get to know guys like Sal when you hang out with guys like Teddy.

"We tutored together," she said. "He was really great with the kids he was tutoring. They all liked him."

I didn't know what to say.

"I wanted to go to the funeral," she said. "But my parents didn't think that was a good idea, you know, with all the talk that's going around. They thought it would upset Sal's parents if I was there. How are they?"

"They're pretty broken up," I said.

Her eyes were watery, like she was going to cry. She turned to go.

"Staci, can I ask you something?" I said. That's when I noticed that Alex had stopped what he was doing and had come down the aisle toward us. He was standing right behind Staci now. She turned and smiled at him.

"Hi, Alex."

Alex's face turned all red. He looked at the floor and mumbled hi to her.

"You better get back to work, Alex, before Mr. Geordi comes by," I said. Mr. Geordi had chewed Alex out twice today already. If Alex hadn't been one of the store's special hires, Mr. Geordi probably would have fired him by now. If Alex kept breaking stuff, he might still get fired.

Alex hesitated—it was obvious he didn't want to go back to where he was supposed to be working. Then his eyes went big. I turned and saw why. Mr. Geordi was standing at the end of the aisle. He looked at me.

"Is there a problem here, Mike?" he said.

"No, sir," I said. "I was just telling this customer where she could find the tomato sauce."

Mr. Geordi's eyes moved to Alex, who immediately ducked his head and retreated up the aisle, where he started putting containers of instant noodles on the shelf again. Mr. Geordi watched him for a moment and then moved on.

"What did you want to ask me?" Staci said.

"It's about the day Sal died," I said. Her eyes got even more watery. "You were with him. You must have seen *something*."

"I told the police everything I know," she said. "But I don't know who killed him."

"You were right when you said Sal and I were close," I said. "He was my best friend. That's why I want to know." I *had* to know. "If you could just tell me what happened . . ."

"It was so stupid," she said. "I don't know why Teddy can't just get over it. But he can't. He goes out of his way to hurt me." She let out a shuddery sigh. "I was going to the mall," she said. "And I saw Teddy and the rest of them up ahead on the sidewalk. I was going to cross the street. Teddy's terrible. Some of his friends are even worse. They used to be my friends, too. But when I broke up with Teddy, some of them acted like I'd broken up with *them*. And Sara D.? She's the worst. She keeps harassing me. She's a real bully. I think she's trying to score points with Teddy." She looked fiercely at me. "Do you have any idea how many days I wanted to stay home from school just so that they couldn't hassle me anymore? I almost stayed home from school that day. I was tired of how they were treating me. And, to be honest, I was kind of scared of Sara. She and a bunch of other girls swarmed me the week before." I wondered if she had seen me watching that time. If she had, she didn't say so. "Maybe I should have stayed home," she said. "Then nothing would have happened."

I wished she had stayed home, too, just like I wished I hadn't told Rebecca that I had forgotten her history book. But I didn't say anything.

"But I didn't stay home," she said. "I went to school. And when I saw Teddy and the rest of them on the sidewalk at lunchtime, I didn't cross the street like I usually do. For once, I got mad. Maybe that was a mistake. Maybe I should have stayed away from them."

I thought about those butterflies Vin had mentioned. It seemed like there were a lot of things that people could have done differently that day—little things that would have made a big difference.

"But I did get mad," she said. "I thought to myself, *No, I'm not going to cross the street. Why should I? I have as much right to be on the sidewalk as they do.* I was tired of the way Teddy was treating me. I was tired of all of them. So I started to walk right past them. Then Teddy started in. At first I ignored him. Then his friend Matt grabbed me. He's such a loser. He started doing some stupid imitation of some of the special ed kids, and he was grabbing me and Sara D. was saying how I must be in love with them, that's why I tutored them. Teddy thought that was pretty funny. He said the way I acted, it looked like I was in love with . . ." She broke off and glanced up the aisle. "I don't want to repeat exactly what he said," she said in a low voice. "It was something mean about Alex. He's one of the kids I tutor. I was so mad when Teddy said that that I slapped him."

So Kim had been right about that.

"Teddy didn't like that. He doesn't like to be shown up in front of his friends. He shoved me. And the next thing I know, Sal's there and he tells Teddy to back off. When that happened, Teddy went nuts. He asked me if I thought my 'new boyfriend' was going to be able to protect me. He's so stupid. Sal and I weren't going out or anything. You know that—you were close to him. Sal and I were just friends. But I didn't tell Teddy that. I didn't think it was any of his business. Besides, he wouldn't have believed me. And by then I just wanted to get away from there. To be honest, I was kind of scared." She looked at me. "It's been bothering me a lot—the fact that I didn't tell Teddy right out that Sal and I weren't seeing each other. Maybe I should have said something. Maybe it would have made a difference."

Maybe.

"Then what happened?" I said.

"Sara D. shoved me. Then Sal grabbed me and put his arm around me. I could see that that made Teddy even angrier. Then Sal started to walk me away from there. Sara D. was yelling things at me. I yelled right back at her. I told her if she ever came near me again, I was going to call the police."

"Then?"

"They were following us, so Sal told me to go across the street, away from them. I asked him, 'What about you?' I looked at him. He had a funny look on his face, like he'd seen something. Like he was scared or something."

"Scared of Teddy, you mean?"

"I guess," she said. "I mean, Teddy was really angry. And he was with a lot of his friends. They all back him up. They always do. I wanted Sal to come with me, but he told me to go ahead. So I did what he said. I was shaking. I crossed the street, and I went back to school. What I really wanted to do was go home. But I can't keep running away from Teddy. Can I?"

"What about Sal? Did Sal cross the street with you?"

"Not that I saw," she said.

"Why not?"

"I don't know. I went into the school, straight to the girls' bathroom. I was shaking so hard. A little while after that I heard that somebody had been stabbed in an alley and . . ." She started to cry now. "I shouldn't have gone to school that day. I should have crossed the street to avoid Teddy. I shouldn't have lost my temper."

"Do you think Teddy did it, Staci?"

"I don't know." She was sniffling, and tears were dribbling down her cheeks. I wished I had a tissue to give her. "The police asked me that," she said. "But I don't know. I went back into the school. I should have made Sal come with me. I should have—"

"It's not your fault, Staci," I said.

A woman who had been studying pickles, trying to decide which kind to buy, gave me a dirty look, like it was all my fault Staci was crying. When Staci finally said, "I'm sorry," and ran down the aisle, colliding with a shopping cart that was just turning the corner, the woman said to me, "You should be ashamed of yourself."

In a way, she was right.

» » »

An hour later, when I was sitting out behind the store, taking my break, Alex came out and said, "You better leave her alone."

"What?" I said.

"I saw what you did. You made her cry. You better leave her alone."

"I was just talking to her, Alex," I said. "She was crying because of the kid who died. Sal. You knew Sal, right?"

"Leave her alone," he said again. He was shifting back and forth on his feet, rocking like a boxer who was getting ready to throw a punch. Why was he so mad? I thought about the way he'd acted in the store when Staci had said hi to him.

Oh.

"You like her, is that it?" I said. "You like Staci?"

Boy, did he ever look surprised, which told me I was right.

"Well, you can relax, Alex," I said. "I'm not interested in Staci that way. I have a girlfriend. We were just talking, that's all."

He thought about that for a moment. "You have a girlfriend?" he said.

"Yeah. Her name is Rebecca."

He thought about that, too. Then he went back into the store.

CHAPTER TEN

By the end of the next day, I felt like I was going to explode again. Teddy wasn't in any of my classes, but I kept seeing him in the hall and in the cafeteria, and the more I saw him, the more worked up I got. I think I would have punched something if I hadn't had gym last period. We finished the class by doing laps. When the bell rang, I asked Mr. Zorbas if I could stay and run some more. He let me. It made me feel better. I ran until I couldn't run any more. Then I showered and went up to my locker to get my stuff.

I saw Mr. Gianneris halfway down the hall. He was holding a cardboard box, and he was standing in front of a locker. Sal's locker. The way he looked at me, you would have thought I'd caught him breaking into it.

"I'm glad you're here, Mike," he said. "It will save me calling you to the office tomorrow morning."

Calling me to the office? Now what had I done?

"I phoned Sal's house to talk to his parents," he said. "I ended up talking to his aunt. His mother was too upset to come to the phone. I can't imagine what they must be going through." He shook his head. "I asked Sal's aunt what his parents wanted to do about Sal's locker. The police have already been through it."

"Are you going to take his stuff over to her?"

"I offered to, but she said no. She asked me if I could give his things to you."

"She wants *me* to take Sal's things over there?" I liked Sal's mom. I really did. But I was kind of afraid to see her again. What would I say?

"Sal's aunt thought maybe you would take the things home, and she'll get them from you when his parents are ready to deal with it. I said I'd ask you."

I didn't feel the same way about Mr. Gianneris as I did about Sal's parents. Mostly I didn't like him. But his voice quivered when he spoke. He couldn't be all that bad if he felt the way he did about what had happened.

"Okay," I said.

He dug in his pocket for a piece of paper. Sal's combination.

"I can do it, if you want," I said.

He nodded and didn't say anything while I spun Sal's combination, even though it was against the rules for students to tell other students their combinations. Everyone did it. Sal knew my combination. So did Rebecca, but she hardly ever used it. Vin used to go into my locker all the time when he was at this school. He used to borrow my textbooks whenever he lost his or forgot them at home. Sometimes he used to copy my homework without asking me. A couple of times he took some stuff from my lunch.

I took the lock off and reached out, but I couldn't do it. I stepped aside and let Mr. Gianneris actually open the locker door.

The first thing I saw—and it surprised me because I hadn't seen them before—were two pictures hanging inside the locker door. One was of Imogen. It looked recent. The other one was older—maybe five or six years old. It was a picture Vin's mom had taken one summer. It showed Sal and Vin and me out in Vin's backyard. We were wearing shorts but no T-shirts, and we were all tanned, but neither Vin or I was as dark as Sal. I was in the middle, and we all had our arms over each other's shoulders. We were all grinning at the camera. Mr. Gianneris glanced at me. He took down both pictures and handed them to me to put in the cardboard box. There was also a mirror on the inside of the locker door, I guess so Sal could check out how he looked, maybe so he'd look good for Imogen. Mr. Gianneris took that out, too, and handed it to me. I put it in the box. He took out all of Sal's textbooks, which he started to pile on the floor because they belonged to the school, not to Sal. He took out Sal's binders and notebooks, which went into the box. The only other thing in the locker that belonged to Sal instead of the school was a sweater. Mr. Gianneris folded it up, and I put it on top of the stuff in the box. Then he took the lock, which I had looped through the little hole in the locker door, and handed it to me to put in the box, too. He closed the locker quietly and bent down to pick up the stack of textbooks.

"Thanks, Mike," he said.

After he'd gone, I went to my locker to get my backpack and the stuff I needed for my homework. That's when I noticed Sal's biology binder on the top shelf. I had borrowed it to copy some notes, and I still had it. I added it to the box that Mr. Gianneris had given me.

I carried the box downstairs. It wasn't heavy. I had just stepped out onto the sidewalk when someone bumped into me, hard, and the box went flying. I heard someone laugh. It was Sara D. She was leaning against a utility pole, grinning and enjoying the stupid surprised look on my face. Then someone else—the man who had bumped into me—said, "I'm sorry. I wasn't watching where I was going."

He bent down at the exact same time as I did to pick up the box.

"It's okay," I said. Jeez. "I've got it."

Well, I had most of it. Some of the notebooks and a bunch of loose papers, plus Sal's sweater, had fallen out. The man bent down to start picking stuff up and looking at it. I grabbed the things out of his hand. Sal's stuff was none of his business. Then I saw the pink envelope from his biology binder on the ground—a stupid love letter from Imogen. The man bent down to pick that up, too, but I got to it before he did and jammed it into the box. He must have realized I was mad because his face got all red.

"I'm sorry," he said again. "I was on my way to the school office before—" He stopped and took a good look at me. "You're Michael McGill, aren't you?"

"Yeah," I said. So what if I was? And who was this guy, anyway?

"I saw you on the news." Not only had I made it into the newspaper after Sal's funeral, but I'd turned up on the TV news, too. Rebecca had seen me. She told me about it. "I'm Gil Anderson," the man said. He reached into his pocket for a business card, which he handed to me. "I work for the community newspaper," he said.

I glanced at the card. I knew the paper he meant. It was a weekly that covered stuff like local soccer tournaments and fundraisers at the hospital, and came stuffed with sale flyers. The newspaper office was down the street from school.

"I'm also a freelance journalist," he said.

I handed the business card back to him.

"I've been following the murder of Sal San Miguel," he said. "I'm doing a piece on youth violence and what can be done to stop it, and I'd love to interview you. You were his best friend, weren't you?" He was talking fast, like he was afraid I'd take off before he finished what he had to say. Well, he had that right. I got a good grip on the box and started to walk up the street.

"Wait," Gil Anderson said. He ran around in front of me and walked backward, peering into my eyes while he talked. "I'm sure you have a lot to say. I'm sure—"

"I don't want to talk to any more reporters," I said.

"I understand how you feel," he said. I wished people would stop saying that to me. "It's one of the hardest things about my job—trying to talk to people after they've been struck by tragedy. Think about it. It doesn't have to be now. It can be any time. I can come by your house, if you want. Where do you live?" When I just looked at him, he said, "We can meet anywhere you want. I know you have something to say about what happened. I just want to include your point of view. Here, take my card." He dropped the business card into the box. "Think about it, and if you feel like it, call me. I wrote my cell phone number on the back. That's the best way to reach me."

I kept walking. For a minute, I thought he was going to follow me and keep trying to convince me. But he didn't. He finally left me alone. When I looked back over my shoulder, I saw him going into the school. Probably he was going to harass some other kids who might have known Sal. Well, good luck.

» » »

I took Sal's box up to my room and dropped it onto my bed. I picked up one of his binders and started to flip through it. Boy, he's always been neat—way neater than me. He had nice handwriting, too. You could actually read it. Vin and I used to tease him about it all the time. We . . .

My eyes started to tear up just thinking about the things we used to do. No wonder his mom didn't want Sal's locker things right away. She had all his other stuff at home—all those things to remind her.

I shoved the box into my closet and went back downstairs. There was a message from Riel saying that he wouldn't be home for supper after all. Susan was working. I could have heated up some leftovers or made myself a sandwich, but I didn't. Instead, I headed over to the McDonald's where Sal used to work. I stood outside for a few minutes, looking at the place and remembering.

"Mike?"

I turned. A girl was coming around the side of the building. It was Tulla.

"You coming inside?" she said.

I hesitated. Maybe this wasn't such a good idea.

"Come on," Tulla said. "I'll get you a pop. Coke, no ice, right?" She took my hand, pulled me inside, and led me up to the counter. The place was quiet—there were a couple of kids about my age at a table on one side of the restaurant and four old guys drinking coffee at a table on the other side, and that was it. "Another fifteen minutes and the place will be jammed with the supper rush," Tulla said. She went behind the counter, grabbed a cup, and started to fill it with Coke. "It's not the same around here without Sal," she said.

While she got my drink, I looked around. There was a framed photograph on the wall. A little metal tag attached to the bottom of it read *Community Spirit Champions*.

"It's from all the money the store raised for charity last year, before I was here," Tulla said, nodding at the photo. "This store beat out every other McDonald's in the city. Mr. Torrence likes to show off that picture even though he had nothing to do with it. He says it shows people that we have a heart. But if you ask me, what it really shows is how much turnover there is here. Sal's the only person from then who's still working here." She realized what she'd said, and her face turned red. "You know what I mean," she said.

I ordered a burger and fries, and while I waited, I took another look at the picture. I only recognized two people—Sal and the girl who was standing right beside him. I remembered her from the ripped picture in Sal's room.

"Who is that?" I said, pointing to her.

"I have no idea," Tulla said. "That was way before my time." She put my burger and fries on a tray. When I reached for my wallet, she said, "It's on the house."

I thanked her, carried my tray to a table, and sat down to eat. Before Sal started working here, Vin and Sal and I used to come to this McDonald's all the time for pop and fries and Big Macs and just to horse around and have fun. Then Sal got a job here, and I used to come in all the time, and he'd come and say hi or sit with me on his break. It got so I couldn't walk past the place without thinking of Sal. It was going to be a long time before I ever came back.

» » »

I was practically running by the time I got to work. In about two minutes I had to be on the floor, and I still had to sign in. I ran around the back to the employee entrance and saw Alex talking to Bailey. Whatever Bailey was saying, he had a serious expression on his face. I wondered if he was giving Alex a hard time. But Alex didn't look like he was being bothered. He just shook his head and said something and went inside.

I had to pass Bailey to get into the store. I kept my eyes straight ahead so that I didn't have to look at him. Seeing Teddy's friends was just as bad as seeing Teddy.

Bailey walked past me without saying a word.

» » »

About an hour into my shift, I was stocking the potato chip aisle when I looked up and saw Staci. She was with a man who was pushing a shopping cart. Staci was walking beside him, talking to him. She nodded when she saw me, but she didn't come over to talk to me. I didn't blame her. I didn't really know her, and we had already talked about the only thing we had in common. The man she was with—I guessed he was her father—grabbed a couple of bags of chips and threw them into the cart. Then he pushed the cart past me. Staci followed him. I was on my way to the stockroom a few minutes later to get a skid of pop when I saw her again, over in the meat section, close to where Alex was setting up a display of the canned chili that was on special. At least, that's what he was supposed to be doing. What he was actually doing was watching Staci. She glanced over at him and flashed a big, friendly smile. Alex's whole face turned red, like he'd been caught doing something bad. He spun around so fast that he banged into the display he had been working on and knocked the whole thing over. Cans of chili crashed to the floor and rolled everywhere. One of them came to a stop at Mr. Geordi's feet. Mr. Geordi bent down, picked it up, and gave Alex an exasperated look. But Alex didn't notice because he had heard the same thing I'd heard—laughter—and he turned toward it. It was Staci. I don't think she meant to laugh. I think it was just an automatic reflex—you know, how you laugh when you see something unexpected, like someone slipping on the ice and trying not to fall. She stopped as soon as she saw the look on Alex's face. She hurried over to him and started picking up cans.

"I'm sorry, Alex," she said. "I hope I didn't hurt your feelings."

Mr. Geordi picked his way through the cans to where Staci was standing. "That's all right, miss," he said. He took the cans she had picked up. "We'll take care of this."

"But I don't—" Staci began.

"We'll take care of it," Mr. Geordi said firmly.

Staci hesitated. "I'm sorry I laughed, Alex," she said again before she went to find her father.

As soon as she was gone, Mr. Geordi started telling Alex that he should be watching what he was doing, what would happen if some old lady tripped on one of those cans and fell and broke her hip, the store could be sued, did he understand what that meant? He was trying not to get mad, but if you ask me, he sounded like he was fed up with Alex always making mistakes. If Mr. Geordi had been in charge of the store, I don't think there would have been any special program to hire people with disabilities. If Mr. Geordi wanted to do something for disabled people, he probably would have just made a donation to a charity.

Alex's face got even redder as he stood there listening to Mr. Geordi.

"You, Mike," Mr. Geordi hollered, snapping his fingers at me. "Get over here and help clean this up before someone gets hurt." The way he said it made me feel that he thought I was somehow responsible.

I started picking up cans and stacking them again.

"You, too, Alex," Mr. Geordi said.

Alex bent down to retrieve a couple of cans, but when he went to add them to the display I was rebuilding, he stepped too close. His foot caught one corner of the base and the whole display collapsed again, sending more cans rolling all over the floor. Mr. Geordi swore. For a minute I thought he was going to fire Alex. But, no, he did even worse. He stood there with his arms crossed over his chest and watched every move that Alex made, which, of course, rattled Alex even more. I scrambled to get the display rebuilt, praying the whole time that Alex wouldn't knock it over again.

When we had finally finished, Mr. Geordi scowled at Alex and barked at me to get back to work.

Right. You're welcome.

At break time, I went into the storeroom and sat on a packing crate to eat a bun that I'd bought from the bakery section and stuffed with sliced meat that I'd bought at the deli counter. I had just bitten into it when Alex came in with a brown paper bag that I guess he'd brought from home. When he saw me, he turned and headed for the door. Jeez, I had helped him out—I was always helping him out—and all of a sudden he was acting like I was the last person he wanted to have lunch with.

"Come on, sit down," I said. I shifted over on the crate.

He hesitated. He seemed to be really thinking about it. But he finally dropped down beside me, opened his bag, and pulled out what looked like a peanut butter and jam sandwich on good old regular sliced white bread. Riel never bought white bread, ever. I watched as Alex took a bite. I couldn't remember the last time I had had a plain (nonorganic) peanut butter sandwich on plain, "no good for you" white bread. It seemed like a whole lifetime ago.

I took a bite of my own sandwich. Riel never bought deli meat, either. He said it was poison. But, boy, did it ever taste good.

"She really has you all shook up, huh?" I said.

"Who?"

"Staci. I saw the way you looked at her."

Alex hung his head. "She laughed at me."

"She didn't mean to. It was just that it was kind

of funny to see that display collapse like that. Even I thought it was funny, Alex, but that doesn't mean I was laughing at you. Besides, Staci apologized, didn't she?"

He looked doubtful.

"She wanted to help you pick everything up, Alex. She would have, too, if Mr. Geordi hadn't stopped her."

"You really think she wanted to help?" He sounded like he couldn't believe it.

"Yeah. She seems nice." Maybe Rebecca was right. Maybe Staci had finally opened her eyes one day, seen what a jerk Teddy was, and decided she wanted something different in her life. Maybe that's why she dumped him.

"She liked that other guy, the one that died."

"They just tutored together, that's all. And, anyway, he was like me. He already had a girlfriend."

"He did?"

"Yeah. He liked Staci as a friend, that's all."

"But Teddy said—" He stopped suddenly and looked down at the floor.

"What did Teddy say?"

He didn't answer.

"You heard Teddy that day in the hall at school, didn't you, Alex? You heard him threaten Sal, didn't you?"

Alex shook his head, but he didn't look at me.

"You heard Teddy tell Sal to keep away from Staci, didn't you, Alex?" He still wouldn't answer. "Did you tell the police that?"

He looked scared when I mentioned the police. I wondered if Teddy had seen Alex in the hall the day he threatened Sal. I wondered if he had sent Bailey to the store to tell Alex to keep his mouth shut.

"Teddy was wrong about Sal and Staci," I said. "They were just friends. You shouldn't believe anything Teddy or any of his friends say. You shouldn't protect them, either."

"I'm not protecting them." But he still wouldn't look at me. I was pretty sure he was hiding something.

"They're a bunch of jerks, Alex. Their idea of a good time is to hassle people. They were hassling Staci just before Sal was killed."

Finally he met my eyes. "What do you mean?"

"They were making fun of her because she tutors. They were making fun of the kids she tutors. That's why Sal went over to help her. Because they were making fun of the kids she tutors, and Staci got mad at them, and things started to get rough."

"Staci tutors me sometimes," Alex said in a soft voice.

"Yeah, well, then I guess that Teddy and Bailey and the rest of them were making fun of you, Alex. So if you're protecting them or—"

"Bailey would never make fun of me," he said.

"Right," I said. "Bailey's your friend."

"He's not my friend," Alex said. "But—"

"If he's not your friend, then what did he want outside?" I said. "I saw him talking to you before work."

"Bailey would never make fun of me," he said again.

"He was out there when it happened, Alex. He was out on the sidewalk the day Sal was killed. He was one of the ones who was hassling Staci."

"No, he wasn't."

"Yes, he was."

"I don't believe you."

"It's what people are saying, Alex."

"People say a lot of things."

"I'm talking about people I know, Alex."

"You don't know anything. You weren't there."

"Neither were you. At least, that's what you told me. But Bailey was there. So was Staci. You can ask her, if you don't believe me. You can ask her what they were saying."

"Bailey would never make fun of people," Alex insisted. "He's not like that. He's not." He gripped his sandwich so hard while he talked that it got all squished. Then he threw it against the wall. His face turned red again, but with rage this time. He stood up and turned to face me. He was breathing hard, and his whole body was tensed. I was pretty sure he was going to hit me. Jeez, he was pretty worked up over a guy he'd just told me wasn't his friend.

"Hey, Alex, relax," I said, trying to keep my voice low and calm. "I'm sorry, okay? Maybe you're right. I mean, I hardly know Bailey. I was just saying what I heard. But you're right. Sometimes people say dumb things. I'm sorry. Okay?"

He kept right on staring at me, but his breathing slowly went back to normal.

"Okay," he said. He sat down beside me again and opened the brown paper bag his sandwich had been in. He pulled an apple out of it and looked at it. Then he looked at the squished sandwich lying on the ground near the wall. He sighed and bit into the apple.

"You really think she wanted to help me?" he said while he chewed.

"Yeah," I told him. "I do. I think if anyone would stick up for you, it would be Staci."

CHAPTER ELEVEN

I couldn't believe it was Friday again, more than one whole week since Sal had been killed, and unless someone was planning to surprise me with some news when I got downstairs for breakfast, the cops still didn't know who had done it.

You would have thought that after all this time I'd be used to the idea of Sal being gone. You would have thought I'd be used to the idea of not seeing him when I got to school. But I wasn't. If anything, it was getting harder and harder to make myself get out of bed in the morning, get dressed, and drag myself to school. Even when Rebecca walked with me, which she couldn't every day because of band practice and because she had gone out for volleyball again this year. I couldn't stand the idea that I might be sitting in a classroom or walking down the hall or standing out on the playing field and that the person next to me or across the room from me or walking past me might be the person who had knifed Sal in the chest. Just the thought of that made me want to punch my fist into a wall. I thought of all the people that the cops must have talked to—that Dave Jones must have talked to—and so far nothing had happened. Whoever had done it was still out there somewhere, walking around, and the cops were none the wiser. I didn't want to go to school.

But I had to.

There was no way Riel would let me stay home. There was no way I could even make myself ask him. And even if I did, he would probably just tell me to suck it up, it's too bad what happened, it's a genuine tragedy, but life goes on. He'd be nice about it. He'd probably do the same thing Rebecca had done. He'd probably tell me I should talk to someone. But that person would probably tell me what I didn't want to hear: life goes on. It always goes on. So I didn't even ask.

Riel looked up from his newspaper when I walked into the kitchen.

"Mr. Gianneris called me at work yesterday," he said. "He says some reporter went to the school office yesterday and asked a lot of questions about you."

"It must be the guy who bumped into me after school yesterday," I said. "He's working on an article on youth violence. He wanted to interview me."

Riel put down his newspaper.

"I told him I wasn't interested," I said, so that maybe he'd lose that sharp look on his face. "And I'm not. What did the school tell him?"

"Nothing," Riel said. "It's against school policy to give out information about students."

"I thought he was going to follow me home or

something," I said. "He really wanted to talk to me."

"At least he can't find you through the phone book. If he bothers you again, let me know, Mike."

The only phone in the house was listed under Riel's name.

I ate some breakfast and then went to school.

I stood outside, and I looked at the faces of all the kids who were standing around out there, waiting for the bell to ring. When I went inside, I looked at the faces of all the kids who were rushing for their lockers. I looked at the faces of all the kids who were hurrying to their homerooms and then who were out in the hall again a few minutes later, hurrying to their first class of the day. I looked at the faces of all the kids in my first class. And my second class and my third. The only thing that made it even the least bit bearable was Rebecca. She was in a couple of my classes, so at least when I looked at her, I knew for sure that she'd had nothing to do with it and, because she hadn't been anywhere nearby, that she hadn't been one of those people who had just stood and watched while everything was happening. But that didn't stop my hands from clenching and my stomach from churning when I looked at all the other people—kids and teachers—who were going through the day like it was any other day, like nothing had happened, like nothing—or no one—was missing. It didn't stop me from wanting to scream at them or grab them and shake them and tell them—*yell* at them—that this wasn't a day like any other day and that someone *was* missing.

Someone important. To me, anyway.

Lunchtime.

Rebecca couldn't go to the cafeteria with me. She had a meeting for her exchange trip.

"I'm sorry, Mike," she said. She'd been apologizing for days now. She apologized when she couldn't walk to school with me. She apologized when she had to meet with some other kids for her biology assignment. She said, "I feel like I shouldn't even be thinking about school. And then I tell myself, I bet Sal wouldn't want everyone to mess up their grades on account of him. Don't you think, Mike?"

I bet she was right, but school was the last thing I cared about. Whether Sal would have wanted it or not, I was definitely messing up *my* grades. I told her it was okay, that she should go and not worry about it anymore. I didn't tell her that I wasn't sure what I was going to do without her. I didn't want her to feel bad.

"Are you working tonight?" she said.

"Six to nine," I said.

She looked disappointed. "It's my last night in town for a whole week. I was hoping we could spend it together."

"We can do something after work," I said. "I'll come over to your place."

"Okay," she said. She kissed me on the cheek and then hurried off to her class meeting.

I went where I usually went at lunchtime, the cafeteria, even though I wasn't hungry. I bought a carton of chocolate milk and looked around to see if there was anyone I wanted to sit with. There wasn't. I spotted a small, empty table at the back of the room. I was heading for it when I realized that I'd have to squeeze by Teddy and his friends to get there. I glanced at Teddy. He was sitting at one end of the table, like he was the father, with all his friends around the long sides like they were his happy little family. He looked right at me. He didn't smirk the way he usually did. Instead, he looked—I don't know—he looked *serious*, I guess. Just for a second, I thought he was going to say something to me. That was enough to make me change my mind and turn around, which is what I was doing when somebody slammed into me, somebody who was in a hurry to get somewhere.

Alex.

I recognized the look on his face. I had seen it a couple of times at the store. He was worked up about something—so worked up that he didn't even seem to realize that he'd slammed into me.

"Hey!" someone howled—a girl at another table who got elbowed in the head when Alex pushed past her, too. Alex didn't stop, he didn't apologize, he didn't even seem to notice her. He bulldozed his way to Teddy's table, grabbed Bailey by the arm, and wrenched him around. Annie, who was sitting next to Bailey, was so startled that she let out a yelp. Everyone turned to see what was going on.

"You lied to me," Alex said.

"What the—" Bailey began. Alex still had Bailey by the arm, and he dragged him up and backward. He was a beefy guy, and either he was stronger than Bailey or he'd caught Bailey by surprise. Either way, Bailey was slow to react. His chair started to topple over. "What's the matter with you, Alex?" Bailey said. His chair crashed to the floor. The only reason Bailey didn't crash with it was that Alex still had him by the arm and was jerking him up.

"You lied to me. You said you would never let people make fun of me. But you were right there when they did, and you didn't say anything. Staci told me."

"Let go of me," Bailey said. Now that he was on his feet, he looked bigger than Alex. Taller, too. It seemed like it should have been easy for him to break free. But Alex held on tight.

"You lied to me."

I glanced at Teddy, who had a puzzled look on his face as he watched what was going on. Matt and Steven stood up. Each one of them grabbed one of Alex's arms to pull him off Bailey. Alex didn't like that. He kicked and struggled. One kick caught Matt right where it hurt the most. Matt's face turned crimson. He retaliated by punching Alex.

"Stop it," Bailey yelled at him. He shoved Matt away from Alex. "Leave him alone."

Matt was hunched over now because of the pain, but when he looked up at Bailey, I could see that he wanted to punch him, too, for defending Alex.

"Go on," Bailey said to Alex, shoving him, too. "Get out of here before you get everyone in trouble."

Alex glowered at him. "You lied to me."

"Get out of here, Alex," Bailey said.

They locked eyes for a few seconds. Then Alex ducked his head. He turned and pushed his way out of the cafeteria, his eyes down the whole time. Everyone watched him go. I glanced at Bailey. He had a sour look on his face, but he didn't say anything. He sat down again, and Annie laid a hand over top of his.

"Stupid retard," Steven said.

Bailey glowered at him. "Why don't you shut up?" he said.

"Jeez, what's eating you?" Steven said.

Annie squeezed Bailey's hand. The way she looked at him when she did it told me that squeeze meant something and that she was trying to calm him down. It also told me that she knew what was going on, even if no one else did. Bailey sat there stone-faced for a few seconds. Then he raised his head and said to Matt and Steven, "You touch him again, and you'll be sorry."

Steven started to laugh. He thought Bailey was kidding.

"Any of you," Bailey said. "Leave him alone."

"Hey, what's your problem?" Matt said.

"He's my cousin," Bailey said. He spat the words at them, but I couldn't tell if he was mad at them for what they had done or mad at what he was telling them. "He's my cousin, okay?" He got up so fast that he knocked his chair over. He bent down, grabbed it, and slammed it onto its feet. Then he stalked away from the table. Annie grabbed her bag and hurried after him.

The rest of them stared after him in stunned silence. Finally Teddy said, "Jeez, why didn't he just say so?"

» » »

I was at my locker right after school, getting my homework stuff together, when someone behind me said, "Hey, McGill."

It was Teddy. I turned slowly and stared at him.

"Are you talking to me?" I said.

"Yeah," he said. For once he wasn't smirking. He had the same look on his face that I'd noticed down in the cafeteria. "Look, about your friend Sal—"

I started to seethe inside. I didn't want to hear him talk about Sal.

"I was pissed at him, okay? I admit it."

But he kept talking. I wanted to lunge at him. I wanted to hit him. I wanted to hurt him.

"Seeing Staci with him, it really got to me," he said.

I wanted to smash his face in.

"Being dumped . . ." He shook his head. "That really messed me up, you know?"

But what good would it do? I forced myself to think about Sal and what *he* would do. He wouldn't smash Teddy—or anyone else—in the face. No way. He would count to ten, and then he would walk away.

I stared at Teddy for a moment and then turned back to my locker. I wanted him to go away, but I didn't hear footsteps, so I knew he was still standing behind me.

"Look, I'm really sorry about what happened," he said. "I know what you think, but I had nothing to do with it."

I could feel my heart pounding in my chest. I could feel myself going cold all over. If he didn't leave me alone—

"The cops believe me, you know," he said, still in a quiet voice. "There are five different guys who said they saw me out there the whole time and that I never left the sidewalk."

Right. Five guys. Five guys who hung around with him all the time. Five *friends*. Talk about credible witnesses.

"It wasn't me," he said. "It wasn't any of us."

I wanted him to leave. But he wouldn't. He just kept standing there, talking to me.

"I know how you feel," he said.

Boy, that was the last thing he should have said to me. I turned around to face him.

"You're probably wishing you hadn't blown him off that day," he said. "Maybe you think it would have made a difference if you hadn't."

It was hard to keep calm. "What are you talking about?" I said.

"I took a look at that note you stuck on his locker."

"You *what?*"

"After I saw what you did—"

"What *I* did?"

"I saw what was in your locker, McGill. I heard you lie to your girlfriend. It made me wonder, you know? So when you went and stuck that note on Sal's locker, I was curious. So I read it."

He never finished what he was saying because I dropped the books I had in my hands and I shoved him back into the bank of lockers on the opposite side of the hall. I slammed him so hard that I must have knocked the wind out of him, because he had a dazed look on his face and his knees buckled. That didn't stop me. I wanted to hurt him. I wanted to hurt him bad for what he had just said. When he started to come off the lockers, I shoved him again, harder this time. This time some kids who were at the far end of the hall turned to look.

"Hey, I just—" Teddy started to say.

I punched him as hard as I could in the stomach. He didn't fight back, and that made me even angrier. I wanted him to fight. I wanted to get into it with him. I wanted to feel something besides all the stuff that was whirling around inside me. I wanted him to come right back at me and make me feel something—*anything*. But he didn't.

I pulled back my fist to hit him again, to see if I could make him at least try to defend himself. But a couple of guys ran down the hall. They weren't even Teddy's friends, but they helped him to his feet. Then one of the guys, a senior, I think, stepped between Teddy and me to keep me from hitting him again. The next thing I knew, Ms. Rather appeared. She looked at Teddy and then at me. She asked Teddy if he was okay, and he said he was, even though he looked kind of pale and shaken up. She looked at him for a few more moments. Then she said, "To the office. Both of you. Now."

I marched down to the office. Teddy must have been moving a lot more slowly because he didn't show up until after I had been sitting on the bench opposite the counter for at least a minute. He sat down beside me but left a big space between us. His face was still pale as he glanced around. We were the only students in the office. There were two secretaries, but they were both on the phone. Right after that Ms. Rather walked in. She came over to where we were sitting and looked at us. She zeroed in on me and said, "Which one of you is going to tell me what happened?"

"It was my fault," Teddy said. "I said something I shouldn't have, and Mike reacted. I'm sorry."

Ms. Rather's eyes shifted from me to Teddy. I held my breath and wondered exactly what Teddy was going to tell her.

"I said something about his friend," he said. "It was stupid, and I'm sorry. I mean, what if my best friend had just died? And what if some ass— What if some*one* said something stupid about the guy? I'd probably do exactly what Mike did."

"That wouldn't make it right," Ms. Rather said. "We expect students at this school to settle their differences without resorting to violence."

"I know," Teddy said. "But people don't always act the way they're supposed to when they're grieving, am I right?"

I glanced at him. Why was he defending me like that?

"Give Mike a break, Ms. Rather," he said. "I promise I won't shoot off my mouth anymore. That way, Mike won't have any reason to get mad. What do you say?"

Ms. Rather looked at Teddy. She looked at me. She said, "So you're telling me that if I let you walk out of this office, you two will get along. No more fighting. Is that it?"

"Yeah," Teddy said.

She looked at me. "Mike?"

"No more fighting," I mumbled.

"Well, why don't we put that to the test?" She leaned back in her chair. "Every time there's a football game or a soccer game—including games played by people who use the playing field but who aren't members of our school community—the spectators leave a big mess behind. You can hardly see the ground under the bleachers for all the candy bar wrappers and popcorn bags and plastic cups. With school budgets the way they are these days, we have fewer caretakers working fewer hours, which means that they can't keep up with everything. No one has had the time to clean up under the bleachers. I was going to make an announcement about that and to ask for volunteers to pick up all the litter. I can see now that I don't have to do that, do I?"

Teddy caught on faster than me. He said, "No, ma'am. I'd be happy to take care of that for you."

Ms. Rather looked at me. When I didn't say anything, Teddy added, "And I'm sure Mike would, too, isn't that right, Mike?"

"Why, thank you, Teddy," Ms. Rather said. "Report to the caretaker's office. I'll call Mr. Wong and let him know you're on your way. He'll give you everything you need to get the job done."

Teddy stood up. So did I. We headed for the door.

"Mike?" Ms. Rather said. I stopped and turned back to look at her. "The first time, Mr. Gianneris gave you a pass. I'm giving you one this time—I won't even tell John—because I think I know where all this hostility is coming from. But it has to stop. This type of behavior won't be tolerated, no matter what's causing it. If you're having problems dealing with what happened to Sal, I can refer you to someone. But it's your responsibility to take the first step. This is the absolute last time that you'll get a break from me or from any other staff member in this school. You get physical with another student for any reason whatsoever and you'll be looking at a three-day suspension. Do you understand me?"

Whatever.

» » »

I went downstairs with Teddy, but not because I was afraid I would get suspended if I didn't. I didn't care. I didn't go because I was afraid that Ms. Rather would tell Riel, either. I just went. Teddy was smart enough not to say anything to me. Mr. Wong, the head caretaker, was on the phone when we got to his office, but he hung up almost immediately and smiled at us.

"I love volunteers," he said.

He showed us where we could get some coveralls and work gloves. Then he showed us where we could find a couple of gigantic plastic garbage cans on wheels, plus some rakes and a couple of poles with big metal spikes on the ends of them.

"Those are to pick up litter," he said, "not to wage mortal combat."

Teddy smiled. I didn't.

"You know the job," Mr. Wong said. "I'll be out in a minute. Ms. Rather wants me to keep an eye on you two."

Ms. Rather wasn't kidding about the mess under the bleachers. Besides candy bar wrappers and drink cups, there were empty cigarette packages, burnt-up matches, empty chip bags, dirty tissues and paper napkins, bus and subway transfers, old newspapers, game lineups, and some other, more disgusting stuff.

Teddy headed over to one end of the bleachers, so I immediately went to the other end. I know it was supposed to be punishment, but the truth was that I didn't mind it. It felt good to stab and *stab* and *STAB* at garbage with those sharp metal spikes. I kept going until there was no more room left on the spike, and then I pushed all the stuff off into the plastic garbage can and started all over again. Bit by bit, the ground under the bleachers started to look good. Bit by bit, Teddy and I worked our way toward each other. The whole time I wondered what exactly he had seen and who he had told—and who he might tell.

Finally, we were separated by only a couple of yards. He looked at me. He seemed tense, on edge, like maybe he thought I might hit him again. But Mr. Wong was at the side of the athletics field. He was watching us.

"I won't tell anyone, if that's what you're worried about," Teddy said, his voice quiet even though there was no one around to hear us. "When someone told me afterward that Sal was supposed to be on his way downtown to write his driver's test, you know what I thought? I thought, *I wish he'd just gone there. Maybe then things would be different.*" He didn't look like the same smirking Teddy now. He didn't look like the guy who was always hassling Staci. "I guess you think the same thing, huh?"

I felt my stomach clench.

"Or if I hadn't mouthed off at Staci again," he said. "Then he wouldn't have had to come and help her. She likes him, you know."

"They were just friends," I said. I wasn't sure why I was even talking to him. "Sal already had a girlfriend."

"That's what he told me. I didn't believe him. Maybe I didn't want to believe him."

What did he mean by that?

"When Staci dumped me, it wasn't even for someone else," he said. "You know what that feels like? You're crazy about this girl. You've been crazy about her forever. And one day, you don't even see it coming, she tells you that's it. She doesn't want to see you anymore."

Why was he telling me this?

"I asked her, did you meet someone else? But no.

That wasn't it. She just didn't want to be with me any-more. Like she was tired of me or something. Then I see her with him, talking and laughing."

As if that were some kind of excuse.

"Look, I had nothing against him, okay? Well, ex-cept that Staci seemed to like him better than she liked me. A *lot* better. But I'm not a killer. I'm not. And I sure didn't want him to die."

I just stared at him.

"I have a big mouth, I admit it. Like at the funeral, with your pal Taglia. I'm sorry about that. We have a little history, him and me." Vin had mentioned that. Teddy looked at me. "The cops really came on strong," he said. "I was scared there for a while. But they believe me. You can ask them. You can get Riel to ask them."

Right, like the cops never got it wrong.

"He was an okay guy," Teddy said. "He was in my history class. He put his hand up a lot. He seemed to get a kick out of getting the right answer. But other than that, he seemed okay. We didn't have any special beef or anything—other than Staci liked to be around him and she didn't like to be around me anymore."

He jabbed the ground with his stick.

"I went into that alley," he said, not looking at me now. "A bunch of us did after that woman came scream-ing out of there."

That cold feeling came over me again.

"I saw him. I guess that's why I went to the funeral." He looked up at me for a moment. Then he jabbed at the ground again. He kept jabbing.

I watched him, and then I joined in. I had never talked much to Teddy—never wasted my time. Never saw any reason to. But looking at him and listening to him just now . . . I wanted to hate him. I wanted to believe it was all his fault. But now I wasn't so sure. Was he telling me the truth, or was he snowing me the way he had maybe snowed the cops?

We finished cleaning up all the mess under the bleachers. Mr. Wong came over to inspect our work. He said we'd been thorough and that we could go.

We went back inside to drop off our coveralls and work gloves. We were going up the stairs when Teddy said, "Hey, do you . . ."

He broke off and shook his head.

Whatever.

He stopped on the step above me. "You want to come to a party tomorrow night?" he said.

I stared at him.

"*You're* inviting *me* to a party?"

"Well, yeah."

"What kind of party? You mean at that construction site?"

"No," Teddy said, surprised. Maybe he didn't know that I'd heard about him and his friends hanging around in those half-built houses. "I mean at the bluffs."

"The bluffs?" What was he talking about?

"Matt's dad lives up there. The guy is loaded. You should see the place. You should see the property. It's huge, and it goes right out to the bluffs. Matt's dad lets him have bonfires out there. The guy ditched Matt's mom for someone half her age, and ever since he pretty much lets Matt do whatever he wants when it's Matt's weekend to stay there. It's great. You want to come?"

"I don't even know Matt," I said.

"So what? The party is for me. It's my birthday. Actually, it was my birthday last week. We were going to have the party last weekend, but it was right after Sal was killed and some of the people I invited knew him. Miranda . . . you know Miranda?" I nodded. "She said it wouldn't be right if kids from school were at a party the day after Sal died."

So that's why Miranda had been talking to Teddy.

"She said I should postpone it. So I did. We're having it tomorrow night instead."

He was really confusing me. He sounded like he meant what he was saying. Or maybe he was a gold-medal liar.

"You want to come? You don't have to buy me a present." He flashed me a smile. I stared at him. "I'm trying to show you I have no hard feelings, McGill," he said.

So he was inviting me to his birthday party? What made him think I would accept the invitation? Why on earth would I want to go to a party for Teddy Carlin?

CHAPTER TWELVE

I had to work that night. When I got to the store, I saw Alex and Bailey at the far end of the parking lot. Bailey was saying something to Alex. When Alex started to walk away, Bailey grabbed his arm and jerked him to a standstill. He looked really angry. I didn't care if they *were* cousins. I started toward them.

Bailey saw me first. He dropped his hand and muttered something to Alex that I couldn't hear. I ignored him and said to Alex, "Are you okay?"

"Yeah," Alex said. He glanced at Bailey, but he didn't seem mad at him the way he had been in the cafeteria. Instead, he seemed kind of sad.

"Remember what I said, Alex," Bailey called after him as Alex and I walked back to the store together.

I waited until we were almost at the employee entrance. I wasn't sure if I should say anything, but I felt bad about what had happened.

"I didn't know Bailey was your cousin," I said. "If I'd known, I wouldn't have said what I did yesterday." At least, I didn't think I would have said it. "I'm sorry if I caused trouble between you two."

"Staci says that she doesn't think Bailey said anything mean," he said. "But he didn't tell them to stop making fun of people. That's wrong. It's wrong." He shook his head.

Yesterday he had been angry with Bailey. Now he seemed disappointed. I guess I would have felt the same way if I'd found out that someone I cared about had let people say all kinds of ignorant, stupid things about me and hadn't told them to just shut up.

"My mom died in the summer," he said. I sure knew what that felt like. "So I had to move in with Bailey and his mom. I know his mom doesn't want me there, but Bailey told her I have no place else to go right now. He helps me with stuff at home, but he says that at school he has his own friends and I should have my own friends."

Oh. So that's what was going on between them. I wondered if Bailey was embarrassed by his cousin. Maybe he thought people would make fun of him if they knew he had a cousin in special ed. I wondered how Alex felt about that.

"Bailey is right," Alex said, as if he knew what I was thinking. "We used to go to the same school in Regina."

"Regina? That's where you're from?"

"Bailey, too. Until his mom and dad got divorced. Then he moved back here with his mom. Kids used to tease me sometimes at our old school. Bailey made them stop."

I guess that changed when Bailey started hanging out with Teddy and his *cool* friends.

"He used to make me stop, too," Alex said.

"Stop what?"

"Stop getting into trouble."

"What kind of trouble?"

"Sometimes I lose my temper," he said. "Then I get into trouble."

I wondered what kind of trouble.

» » »

Work was pretty normal that night—I spent my shift stacking stuff on the shelves. Every now and then I had to run back to the storeroom to tell Mr. Geordi that there was a customer asking if we were all sold out of whatever special was on this week but that wasn't going to be on special come tomorrow morning. If it turned out we weren't sold out, I'd bring the customer whatever it was they were looking for. If we were sold out, I'd have to go back and tell them, "Sorry."

It was maybe five minutes before the end of my shift when I turned around and saw Rebecca standing behind me with a great big smile on her face.

"I thought we were going to meet at your place," I said.

"I finished packing, so I thought I'd come and get you," she said. "We can stop by the video store on the way home and get some movies. My parents are out to-night, Mike. We have the whole place to ourselves."

I like it when Rebecca's parents go out. In fact, some of my best times with Rebecca have been when we rented some movies and it was just the two of us in the house.

"I gotta go sign out," I told her. "I'll be right back."

» » »

My Friday night curfew is usually eleven o'clock. Sometimes—rarely—Riel will extend it to midnight, if I ask. I called him around ten to ask. I was thinking he'd say no, on account of what happened at the funeral. But he surprised me. He said, "Twelve thirty at the latest, okay, Mike?" I didn't ask why he was giving me so much time without an argument. I just said, "Okay."

I had a great time with Rebecca that night. Her parents still weren't home by the time I had to go. She walked me to the door.

"I'm going to miss you, Mike," she said just before she kissed me.

"I'm going to miss you, too," I said, when she finally stopped kissing me.

I thought about her all the way home.

» » »

After work on Saturday, I walked over to the Blockbuster on Danforth to return the movies that Rebecca and I had watched the night before. Teddy and Sara D. and some of the others were standing outside the dollar store next door when I came out. Teddy saw me and nodded at me. Matt saw him do it. He looked confused. Then Sara D. said, "Look who's coming."

It was Staci. She was walking down the sidewalk with a Shoppers Drug Mart bag in one hand. She hesitated when she saw Teddy. I remembered what she had told me about the day Sal had died. I wondered if she was doing the same thing now, if she was trying to decide if she should cross the street to avoid Teddy or if she should stand up for herself. Finally she pulled herself up even straighter and held her head high, like a little bird puffing up its feathers so that it would look bigger than it really was. She began to walk past them.

"Hey, Staci, where—" Sara D. started to say. The snotty look on her face matched the snotty tone in her voice.

Teddy cut her off. He said, "Leave her alone." Sara D. stared at him. She shut right up. Teddy watched Staci as she made her way past him. For once, he didn't say a word. None of them did, although it looked like Sara D. really wanted to. I could see that Staci was relieved. She also seemed a little stunned, like she couldn't figure out what had just happened.

I thought about that all the way home from the video store. I was still thinking about it when I was nuking leftovers for my supper. Susan was working. She said that Saturday nights were the worst nights in the emergency room, especially after ten o'clock. Sometimes she didn't get home until late Sunday morning. Riel was out, too. I sat in front of the TV, eating my supper and thinking about Teddy's party. I thought about what I had seen outside Blockbuster and what Teddy had said he'd seen in that alley. I also thought about what he had seen me do at school the morning Sal died. Then I thought about who would be at Teddy's party—all those kids who had been out there on the sidewalk that day. Maybe one of them had seen something or heard something or knew something. If they had, they sure wouldn't come up to me at school and tell me. I wasn't friends with most of the people Teddy knew. But if I was at the party, and if everyone knew that Teddy had invited me to come ...

I thought and I thought.

Finally, I got up, left a note for Riel—*Gone to see a movie*—grabbed a jacket and headed for the bluffs.

It was dark by the time I got there. I had to take the subway, then a bus, then I had to walk for fifteen minutes along a winding road where the houses were set way back. Finally I found the address I was looking for. The street number was on a stone column to one side of the driveway. There was a big stone fence along the whole front of the property, and the driveway went back a long way until it finally reached a four-car garage. To one side of the garage was a huge house, bigger even than some of the houses in the neighborhood around the private school where Rebecca's mother teaches. Jeez, I never thought that anyone who went to my school would have parents who were so loaded. Well, one parent. Teddy had said that the house belonged to Matt's dad and that Matt's parents were divorced.

I walked slowly up the driveway. Before I left home, I'd thought this was a good idea. But now that I was here, I wasn't so sure. What if Teddy had been playing me?

What if everything he'd said out in the schoolyard had been an act? What if he'd invited me so that he could play a trick on me or make fun of me or humiliate me the way he did Staci? What if he wanted to get back at me for hitting him or because I was friends with Sal? I almost turned around and went back down the driveway. But all of a sudden a voice to my right said, "Hey, you came."

Teddy.

He had just come out a door at the side of the house—a big sliding glass door in a whole wall of glass—and was carrying a big Styrofoam cooler. He grinned at me like he was glad to see me.

"Come on," he said. "I'll show you where the action is."

I hesitated. But, what the hell, I was here, wasn't I? I fell into step beside him. We crossed a patio next to a swimming pool and a hot tub—"Cool, huh?" Teddy said—and then walked uphill until, all of a sudden, I saw fire. We were at the top of a rise in the property. The house was behind us. Up ahead was a huge lawn bordered by trees and bushes. Near the back of the property, which ended at the bluffs, was a huge fire pit with a fire in it and kids sitting all around, laughing and talking and listening to music and drinking and eating. Beyond that was nothing but sky and, way down below, water. I knew there was a marina down there somewhere, but I couldn't see it from where I was standing.

"Come on," Teddy said.

I followed him to the fire. As soon as he set down the

cooler, kids started to get up and come over and grab a cold drink. Teddy made sure everyone knew I was there. A few kids nodded at me. Some of them said hi. A lot of them ignored me. Matt was one of those people, which made me feel awkward because it was his house.

"Here," Teddy said. He handed me a can of pop. "Come and sit down." He led me over to the fire and dropped down on the ground next to Sara D. He put his arm around her, which surprised me because I thought he was still interested in Staci, even though she had dumped him, and because he had stopped Sara D. from giving Staci a hard time today. "Say hi to Mike," he told her. She looked sullenly at me and mumbled a greeting. If you ask me, she was thinking about what had happened at the funeral.

Teddy started talking, telling me about the great parties they had up here when Matt was staying with his dad, and how cool Matt's dad was—he let them do whatever they wanted because, "Get this, Mike, he thinks we're going to do stuff anyway and that it's better if we do it where we can't get into an accident or get busted or anything. The guy is unbelievable. You have to meet him."

While I listened, I looked around. I recognized almost everyone who was there. They almost all went to my school, and they almost always hung out with Teddy. Then I spotted two people sitting far away from the fire. I had to focus hard before I finally made out who they were—Bailey and Annie. They were talking, and Annie was shaking her head, like she was telling Bailey no, no, no.

Teddy kept offering me things to drink and eat, and the music was pretty good, although I couldn't figure out how they could play it that loud without any of the neighbors complaining. Then Teddy looked around and nodded at a girl who was sitting on the other side of the fire. The girl got up, circled around to where I was, and sat down beside me. I recognized her, too. Her name was Meghan. She smiled at me and said she was sorry about what had happened to my friend, which is exactly how she put it—not *Sal* but *my friend*.

Before I could say anything—and I had no idea what to say—I heard an angry noise. I turned toward it. Everyone did. Bailey was standing now, his arms up in the air. He was shaking his head and saying to Annie, "You said you did. You said so." At first Annie was sitting down, but she jumped to her feet and ran away from him.

"Uh-oh," Meghan said. She got up and went after Annie.

Bailey watched her. He seemed to hesitate, like he was trying to decide whether he should chase after them. Finally he turned and walked toward the fire. That's when he saw me and, let me tell you, that stopped him in his tracks. He looked at me. Then he searched out Teddy and gave him a look that said, *What the hell?*

A few minutes later I saw Meghan walking back to the fire alone.

Bailey intercepted her. "Where is she?" he said.

"She went inside."

Bailey started toward the house, but Meghan caught him by the arm.

"She doesn't want to talk to you right now, Bailey. She just wants to chill, okay? She said she'll come back out again in a little while. Okay?"

Bailey stared up the slope. Only the top floor and the roof of the house were visible from where we were. Finally he turned and walked away from the fire to the edge of the bluffs. Meghan dropped down beside me again.

"Poor Annie," she said. "She just hasn't got over it yet. She told me she's been having nightmares about it."

"About what?" I said.

"About what happened." She looked at me as if of course I should know. But I didn't. "After that woman came screaming out of the alley, Annie was the first one to go and see what was going on. She was the first one to see your friend. She said his eyes were still open. She said she thought for a couple of seconds that he was alive."

I felt sick as I pictured it.

I sat there beside Meghan for a long time, listening to her talk about what had happened, which is the way she always said it, not *the kid who got killed* or *your friend that got killed*, but *what had happened* and *how awful it was* and *how she never knew anyone her own age who had died.*

I did. I knew Robbie Ducharme.

After she talked about that for a while, she started asking me about school and which options I was taking and what I thought I was going to do after high school. She said she wanted to be a marine biologist; she said biology was her all-time favorite subject, which surprised me. I'd never figured on any of Teddy's friends doing anything serious, for sure not marine biology. The whole time she was talking, I kept looking up at the house and wondering about Annie and what she had seen. I wondered if the cops had talked to her and, if they had, what she had told them. After a while, a couple of girls got up and started dancing. Then more girls got up and danced. Some of them dragged boys to their feet. The boys mostly just shuffled around, although there was this one guy—he was really into it and, boy, could he move. Soon almost everyone was on their feet.

Meghan pulled me up and started to dance around in front of me, but I don't dance much. I'm not good at it, and I feel stupid doing it. But Meghan didn't seem to notice. She could have been dancing with anyone or no one, I don't think it would have made any difference to her. So while she twirled around, I slipped over to Teddy and said I needed to use the can. He nodded toward the house.

"You sure it's okay?" I said.

"Sure I'm sure," he said.

I jogged up the slope and back down the other side and let myself in through the sliding door that Teddy had come out of. I found myself in a big room filled with leather furniture and lined with bookcases and CD towers. There was a fireplace on one wall and the biggest flat-screen TV I had ever seen on another. But there was no Annie. At least, I didn't see her at first. Then I heard a little sound, like sniffling, coming from the other side of the room, and I froze. Maybe it was her. But what if it wasn't?

I tiptoed toward the sound. There was definitely someone there, and she was definitely crying. I hesitated.

Finally, "Are you okay?" I said.

She must have been curled up in one corner of the couch, because all of a sudden her head popped up. It was Annie. She took a quick swipe at her eyes with a tissue, and at first it looked like she was going to yell at me. But I guess I wasn't who she expected, because she looked from me to the sliding door behind me and then back to me again.

"I came in to use the bathroom," I said. "I heard something. I'm sorry."

She didn't say anything. She just stared at me while her eyes filled with tears again.

"Are you okay?" I said again.

"I keep thinking about him," she said. "About Sal. He was in my chemistry class."

"Someone told me you were one of the first kids in the alley," I said.

Tears ran down both cheeks. She wiped them away, but more kept coming as she nodded.

"I keep seeing him lying there," she said. Her lips started to tremble. "He was looking up. He was looking right at me."

I felt myself shaking. I told myself that the more I talked about it, the longer it was going to take for all those terrible thoughts and all those awful pictures in my head to finally go away. But she had been there. I had to ask her. I had to know.

"Did you see anything else?" I said.

She was staring off into space. If you ask me, she was still seeing it.

"The knife," she said. "I saw the knife. It was lying there right beside him."

"The knife?" I said. I knew Sal had been stabbed. But this was the first I'd heard that whoever did it had left the knife in the alley beside him.

"It was big," she said. "The blade must have been this long." She showed me with both hands. "It looked like a switchblade, but a big one, with a black handle that had a skull and crossbones on it and some numbers."

"Numbers?"

"Three sixes or three nines. I guess it depends which way you hold it. And there was another mark on it. An X. It looked like someone had scratched it into the handle."

"And it was lying beside him?"

"Right beside him. I saw it, and I took out my phone. It was just automatic, you know? I forgot that that woman had run down the street and that there were all those cops there. So I took out my phone and I called 911. And then other people started coming into the alley, and I was afraid someone was going to touch the knife, so I covered it with my scarf. B—" She broke off abruptly.

"But what?" I said.

She looked at me as if she was seeing me for the first time.

"I don't want to talk about it anymore," she said. "I already talked to the cops."

"But they haven't arrested anyone yet," I said. "So if there's anything you maybe forgot to tell them—"

"I told them what I know," she said. "I covered the knife with my scarf even though—" She stopped again.

"Even though what?" I said.

Nothing. She wouldn't even look at me now.

"What made you go into the alley, Annie? I heard that woman was screaming when she came out of there. Weren't you afraid?"

The question seemed to startle her. "What?"

"What made you go into the alley? Did you hear something? Did you see something?"

Her eyes got sharp, and tears stopped leaking out of them.

"You live with Mr. Riel," she said. "I heard he went back to being a cop. You live with a cop. Is that why you're asking me so many questions? Are you working for the cops or something?"

"No." Jeez, why would she say something like that? "No, nothing like that. But, Annie, if you know anything you haven't said . . ."

She looked me directly in the eyes, and if you ask me, she was thinking about it. She was thinking about what I was saying. She opened her mouth to speak, and I held my breath. I was sure she knew something. I was sure she was going to tell me.

Then I heard something behind me—it was the glass

door sliding open. Annie's eyes skipped from me to the door, and her whole body tensed up. I turned and saw Bailey step inside. He scowled at me and crossed quickly to where Annie was sitting.

"Meghan said you were in here," he said. His voice was soft when he talked to her, but when he looked at me again, his eyes were as hard as granite. He glowered at me and then turned to Annie again. "Are you okay?" he said gently.

She started to cry again. She said, "I want to go home." Bailey sat down beside her, put an arm around her, and pulled her close. She let him.

"Annie, he was my best friend," I said.

"Annie doesn't want to talk to you," Bailey said. "Do you, Annie?"

She answered his question by wrapping her arms around him. Bailey stared at me for a moment. Then he turned back to Annie, and they sat there with their arms around each other. There was no way she was going to talk to me now.

I left the house and went back to the fire. The party had really livened up while I was gone, and no wonder. Someone was passing around a bottle. When it got to me, I hesitated. Part of me wanted it. Part of me thought that maybe if I drank some of it, I would forget stuff that I didn't want to think about and I would feel better. Maybe I would, too, for a little while. But the stuff I didn't want to think about, the things I wanted to forget, would be gone for an hour or two at the most. In the meantime, I would get into trouble with Riel. To be honest, part of me didn't care about that. Part of me was still tempted. But there was a whole other part of me, the part that admired Sal for the way he always handled things, even when they were hard, and that said, no, doing something stupid is doing something stupid, no matter how you look at it. Besides, I didn't need any more grief in my life. So I shook my head, and the guy who was holding the bottle passed it to the guy on the other side of me, who turned out to be Teddy. He took it and grinned at me and took a big swallow.

"I gotta go," I said.

"The party's just getting started."

I hesitated. "Teddy, about what you saw at my locker . . ."

"Don't worry, Mike. I said I wouldn't tell, and I won't."

» » »

I got home before either Riel or Susan. I went straight up to my room and got ready for bed. Then I lay there, staring at the ceiling and seeing Sal's face.

CHAPTER THIRTEEN

Riel was in the kitchen when I finally got out of bed the next day.

"You working today?" he said.

I shook my head.

"How about coming outside when you've had something to eat? You can help me clean up the yard."

You could hardly see the grass out back or out front anymore. It was covered with leaves. I said okay. I ate some cereal, grabbed a jacket, and went outside. Riel was cleaning the flowerbeds. He had told me most of the flowers were already there when he bought the house. The same with the raspberry bushes. But it meant he had to spend a lot of time taking care of everything, and he made me help him. When I went outside, he gestured to a rake leaning up against the fence. I started raking all the leaves into a big pile. When I had finished, I used the rake as a shovel and shoveled the leaves into huge brown paper bags so that they could be picked up by the city. By the time I had finished, Riel had done everything he wanted to in the flowerbeds.

"Come on," he said. "It won't take long to do the front."

The front yard was a lot smaller than the backyard.

"I talked to this girl who went into the alley that day," I said.

"What girl?"

"A girl from my school. She was the first one to go into the alley after that woman came running out. She saw Sal. She said she saw the knife."

Riel didn't say anything.

"Why do you think whoever did it left the knife there?" I said. I had been thinking about that ever since Annie told me about it. "Why didn't they take the knife with them?"

Riel still didn't say anything. But that was okay because I had more to say.

"If Sal got killed because of what happened on the sidewalk, if someone chased him into the alley or something like that and then stabbed him, it would be a heat-of-the-moment kind of thing, don't you think? And it was a cool day, but not cold enough for people to be wearing gloves. So if someone stabbed Sal just like that, in the heat of the moment, there would be fingerprints on the knife, wouldn't there?"

"What are you trying to say, Mike?"

"If there were fingerprints on the knife, couldn't you just take fingerprints off everyone who was out there that day and compare them to the fingerprints on the knife?"

Riel looked at me for a moment before he said, "You're assuming there are any unidentified fingerprints on the knife."

"Knives can be traced, can't they? This girl who saw the knife, she described it to me. It sounds like the kind of knife you'd remember if you saw it. Why don't the police let everyone know what the knife looks like and ask if anyone recognizes it?"

"If they thought it would help, they might do that," Riel said.

"Why wouldn't it help? Why don't they just ask the newspapers to publish a picture of it?" Wait a minute. I looked at him. "You said I was *assuming* there are any unidentified prints on the knife. What do you mean? That there were prints on the knife and you *know* whose they are?"

"Mike, you know I can't—"

Right. He couldn't tell me anything.

I took the rake and another big brown paper bag and went around the front to rake the leaves there. Riel followed me, but he didn't say anything.

» » »

When I came downstairs the next morning before school and glanced at the newspaper that was open on the table, my stomach did a flip. Sal's face was staring out at me.

"Did they make an arrest?" I said.

Riel shook his head.

"The police are appealing to parents," he said.

"Parents?"

"Parents of kids who go to school in the area. It's in the newspaper, and it'll be on TV today, too."

"What do the cops expect parents to do?"

Riel pushed the newspaper closer to me. I read the article. It said that the cops were investigating Sal's murder and that it was possible that a student or some students from my school were involved. It said if there was more than one student involved, there were probably different degrees of responsibility for what happened, and that parents should be alert to signs that maybe *their* child was involved. Then it asked a bunch of questions: The day it happened or the day after it happened, was your child being secretive about phone calls he or she made or received? Did your child have several friends over the night that it happened and did they lock themselves in your child's room or the basement and did they act like they didn't want anyone to hear what they were saying? Did your child change his or her clothes when they came home that day for no reason? Did you notice any unexplainable stains that might have been on their clothing in the laundry? Was your child unusually quiet?

"It doesn't mention the knife," I said. "They're asking all these questions. Why didn't they show a picture of the knife or at least describe it and ask parents if they've ever seen their kid with a knife like it?"

Riel didn't say anything.

"How stupid are the cops anyway?" I said, shoving the paper away. "This is the perfect time to ask about the knife."

Something about the expression on Riel's face stopped me from saying any more. I thought about the newspaper article. I thought about what they were asking and what they hadn't asked. I remembered what Riel had said yesterday—that I was assuming there were no unidentified prints on the knife that Annie had seen lying next to Sal in the alley. I had wondered what that meant. Now I thought I knew. There *were* fingerprints on the knife, and the police knew whose prints they were. They were asking parents all kinds of things about their kids and their clothes, but they hadn't asked if they recognized the knife in the alley? Why not? I looked at Riel. They hadn't asked because they already knew whose knife it was, the same as they knew whose prints were on it. I thought back to what Dave had asked me the very same day it had happened: *Did you ever see Sal with a weapon of any kind?*

"The knife they found in the alley," I said slowly. "It belonged to Sal, didn't it?"

Riel looked at me for a few moments before he said, "Yes."

"And the prints on it, they were Sal's," I said.

Riel hesitated again but finally nodded.

"So that knife wasn't the one that killed him," I said. That's why the police didn't describe it. It was Sal's knife. And it wasn't the murder weapon."

But what was that look on Riel's face?

"Was it the knife that killed him?"

Silence.

I felt sick.

"Sal was killed with his own knife?" I said.

"I'm sorry, Mike," Riel said.

"But how? Why?"

Riel hesitated again. His expression was grim as he said, "This stays between you and me, right?"

I nodded.

"It looks like Sal was trying to defend himself," Riel said. "From the prints on the knife and from the wounds . . . it looks like maybe he took the knife out to defend himself and whoever killed him turned the knife against him."

"I don't get it," I said. "Wouldn't there be finger-prints?"

Riel handed me a butter knife and told me to stand up.

"Hold out the knife," he said, "as if you were trying to protect yourself."

I did what he said. He wrapped his hands around my hand and twisted the blade around so that it was pointed at me. I stared at it, then at him. I started to shake all over, imagining what had happened in that alley.

"What was Sal even doing with a knife?" I said.

Riel shook his head.

"Teddy can be a jerk, but he's not scary enough to make anyone carry a knife," I said. At least, I didn't think he was. Sure, he had been mad about seeing Staci and Sal together. But after what he'd told me in the schoolyard, I was pretty sure he hadn't had anything to do with what had happened to Sal. "It doesn't make any sense," I said.

"I have to agree with you," Riel said. "Sal was a good kid. He wouldn't carry a knife unless he had a reason—a *good* reason. If we could figure that one out, maybe we would get somewhere." He glanced at the clock on the stove. "You'd better get going. You're going to be late for school. And Mike? I wasn't kidding. You know you can't tell anyone any of this, right?"

"Yeah." I looked down at the newspaper again. "Do you think this is going to do any good?"

"It's worth a shot." He put his coffee mug into the sink. "I have to go."

» » »

Rebecca called that night to ask me how I was and to see if there was anything new. I wanted to tell her about the knife, but I had promised Riel I would keep my mouth shut. So instead I told her about the appeal that the police had made to parents.

"I wish I hadn't come on this trip," she said. "I wish I was with you."

"You did the right thing," I told her. "But I'll be glad when you're back."

There was a moment of silence on the other end of the phone. Then Rebecca said, "Mike?"

"Yeah?"

More silence.

"Never mind," she said. "It can wait until I get home."

"What? Tell me."

"No. I think it would be better if I waited."

I didn't like the sound of that. "Did you meet a guy there?" I said. "A French guy?"

"I've met lots of French guys," she said with a little laugh. "But none of them are as cute as you. I miss you, Mike. I'll see you Saturday morning. Will you come and meet the bus?"

I said I would. And I felt better that she had asked me. But I still wondered what she wanted to say to me.

» » »

The phone was ringing when I came through the door on Tuesday night after work. I thought it would be Riel, calling to tell me when he was going to be home.

It wasn't.

It was a girl. Staci. She said she had to see me—right away.

"What's going on?" I said.

"Can you please just come?" she said. "It's important."

I hardly knew her. Why was she calling me? What could be so important?

"Is it about Sal?" I said.

"Please come," she said. "You know those new houses they're building down near where the racetrack used to be? I'm down there."

That was where Teddy and his friends liked to hang out. What was she doing there? What was going on?

She told me exactly where she would be waiting.

"Will you come?" she said.

I said okay. But I had a weird feeling about it. Why couldn't she just talk to me over the phone? And why was she down where they were building those houses? So many kids fooled around down there—not just Teddy and his friends—that the developer whose site it was had hired extra security guards. If I went down there and got into trouble with a security guard, Riel would never let me hear the end of it. But I knew Staci wouldn't have called me unless it was something important— something about Sal.

» » »

Staci was exactly where she had told me she would be.

"Come on," she said when she saw me. She took off down an unpaved street. There were houses on both sides, but they weren't ready to live in yet. None of them had windows or doors. A couple had roofs, but the roofs weren't shingled yet. They were mostly just shells of houses, and some of them weren't even that.

"Where are we going?" I said.

She didn't answer. Instead, she waved for me to keep following her, so I did.

She ducked between two just started houses and kept going until she reached the house behind them. This one had a roof on it and windows, but no brick on the outside yet and no doors. Staci walked right in.

"Hey," I said. I could hear Riel's voice in my head:

That's trespassing, Mike, and trespassing is against the law.

It was dark inside. I couldn't see anything. Staci took one of my hands.

"This way," she whispered. She led me deeper into the house. My eyes started to adjust. We were headed for stairs that led down to the basement. "There's no railing," she said. "So be careful."

I followed her cautiously down the stairs. When I got about halfway down, I saw a light.

"It's okay, Alex," Staci said. "It's me. Mike's here with me."

Alex? What was going on?

Once I got to the bottom of the stairs, I saw Alex huddled in the corner of the basement, which was just one big open space with cinder-block walls and a concrete floor. His left leg was twitching, and he was holding a flashlight, which he shone in my eyes, blinding me.

"Hey!" I said.

The beam danced away from my face. Staci had taken the flashlight from Alex. She stood it on its end so that it lit the place up enough for us to see each other. I looked at her.

"What's going on?" I said.

"Alex called me," she said. "I know he likes you. He says you've helped him a lot at work. And I know you live with Mr. Riel. I had him for history last year. He seems like a good guy. So I thought maybe you could talk to Alex and then maybe talk to Mr. Riel. I thought he might know what to do."

"About what?" I said.

"Alex is scared."

I looked at him. He was still crouched down in the corner, like he was trying to make himself melt right into the cinder blocks.

"What are you scared of, Alex?"

"My aunt called the police," Alex said. "She thinks I killed that guy."

"You mean Sal?"

He nodded. I glanced at Staci. She just shook her head.

"Why would your aunt think that, Alex?" I said. But I was starting to feel cold all over, and not just from the night. I remembered how angry Alex had been when he'd seen me talking to Staci. Maybe he'd seen Sal with her. Maybe that had made him angry, too. He hadn't known until I told him that Sal already had a girlfriend. What if . . . ?

"She read something in the paper," Alex said. "She thinks I did it."

"Read something in the paper?" He must have meant that article directed at parents. "But what would make her think *you* did it?"

"She found my clothes. She saw all that blood. She was screaming at me, What have you done, Alex? She called the police."

I stared at him.

"His aunt tried to lock him in the basement until the police got there," Staci said. "But he got away from her. He ran. He called me. He said he needed help. He was crying."

My head was spinning. I felt like I couldn't breathe. Was he really saying what I thought he was saying?

"There was blood on your clothes?" I said.

Alex nodded. He looked miserable.

"Whose blood?"

"That guy who died."

Now my head felt like it was going to explode.

"Your clothes had *Sal's* blood on them?" I said slowly, forcing myself to stay as calm as I could, which wasn't very calm. "How did Sal's blood get on your clothes?"

"When I went into the alley, I saw him lying there," Alex said. "There was blood everywhere—"

"You said you were in school when it happened," I said. "You said you didn't even go outside. Now you're saying you were in that alley?"

He hung his head.

"I was in the hall at school. I looked out the window, and I saw Staci," he said. "I wondered what she was doing, where she was going." He glanced at her and looked embarrassed. "Sometimes if I see she's going to the mall, I go, too," he said softly.

I looked at Staci. She looked embarrassed too.

"Then what did you do, Alex?" I said. I was shaking all over now.

"When I got outside, I saw she was with that guy."

"With Sal, you mean?"

He nodded. "He had his arm around her."

"Is that why you did it?" I said. "Because Staci was with Sal and he had his arm around her?" I remembered him saying that Bailey sometimes had to stop him when he lost his temper because when he was angry, he got into trouble. I had wondered what kind of trouble he meant. "Were you jealous? Is that it, Alex?"

"No," he said. "He said something to her. Then she ran back across the street into the school. She ran right past me, and I saw that she was crying. I was mad at him for making her cry. I wanted to tell him not to do that."

"You thought he hurt her, is that it?" I said. "Is that why you killed him?"

"I didn't kill him!"

He jumped to his feet. I braced myself. I remembered how angry he had been at the store when he didn't want to believe what I had said about Bailey.

"I thought he did something to make her cry," Alex said. "So I wanted to talk to him. I saw him go into the alley so I ran across the street and followed him. When I got there, he was lying on the ground. His eyes were open—"

No. *No.*

"—and he was trying to say something. So I knelt down and there was all this blood coming out of him—"

No.

"You were going to hurt him, weren't you, Alex? He pulled a knife, is that it?" Alex looked a lot stronger than Sal. "You stabbed him with it, didn't you? You killed him."

"No," Alex said. "I knelt down. I was trying to hear what he was saying—"

"Sal," I said. "His name was Sal."

"I tried to hear what he was saying, but he stopped talking. Then Bailey told me—"

Bailey?

"Bailey was there?"

"He came into the alley and saw me. When he saw the blood, he told me to go home right away. He said to try and not let anyone see me. He said I should change and get rid of my clothes. So I did. I was afraid to put them in the garbage because of the raccoons."

The raccoons? I glanced at Staci.

"Raccoons get in the garbage sometimes," she said. "They spill everything all over the place."

"So I hid them in the basement," Alex said. "I hid them good, but my aunt found them."

"Running away like that and hiding clothes with blood all over them—people who haven't done anything wrong don't do things like that, Alex," I said.

"I *didn't* do anything wrong. There was blood on my clothes because I knelt down to hear what he was saying. I told Bailey that. I didn't hurt him. It must have been that man."

"What man?"

"I don't know," Alex said.

"You don't know?" I was practically yelling at him now. "You just said there was a man."

"When I went in the alley, I saw a man running away. I ran around the corner and that guy... Sal... was lying on the ground."

"What man?" I said again.

"Just a man," Alex said. "I didn't see his face. I only saw his back. He had black hair. And he was wearing a dark jacket with a red stripe across it. He—"

I froze. I held up my hand so that Alex would stop talking. I grabbed the flashlight and shut it off.

"Hey," Staci protested.

"I heard a car," I whispered. "Maybe it's a security guard."

We sat in the darkness in silence. I heard footsteps outside. Then I heard them above us. Someone was in the house.

"Alex?" a voice called. "Alex, are you in here?"

"Bailey!" Alex called. Relief flooded his face. "Bailey, I'm down here."

"Come on up, Alex," Bailey said. "It's dark in here. I can't see. Come up here so we can talk."

Alex started up the stairs.

I heard more footsteps overhead.

Bailey wasn't alone.

"Come on," I said to Staci. We made our way to the stairs. Alex reached the top before I put a foot on the first step. I heard him yell. Then I heard someone say, "Alex Farmington, you are under arrest for the murder of Salvatore San Miguel . . ."

CHAPTER FOURTEEN

I had faced a loaded gun once before, but that didn't make it less scary this time. When I climbed up out of the basement, I saw that the unfinished house was filled with cops. I guess they were surprised to see Staci and me because they reacted by pointing their guns at us. I raised my hands, fast.

"Mike," a voice said. It was Dave Jones. "What are you doing here?" He glanced at Staci. He didn't ask her for her name, but I guess he didn't have to. She had told me that she'd spoken to the police about the day Sal died. She'd probably spoken to Dave.

Bailey was there, too, with a woman who I guessed was his mother. They were escorted out of the house. Dave waved over another plainclothes cop to take Staci aside and talk to her.

"Mike?" Dave said again. He was waiting for my answer. So I told him that Staci had called me. "You're going to have to make a statement, Mike," Dave said. I said okay. I also said that I wanted to call Riel. I was afraid he'd get home before I did and that he'd wonder where I was. Riel didn't like to wonder about things like that.

Riel was waiting at the police station when I got there. He stayed with me while I told Dave everything that Alex had told me.

"Alex says Sal had already been stabbed when he got to him," I said. "He says he saw a man running out of the alley." I gave him the description that Alex had given me. "Do you think it's true?" I said. "Do you think the man he saw is the one who killed Sal?"

Dave looked at Riel. He didn't answer. He thanked me for coming in and talking to him.

"What do *you* think?" I asked Riel on the way home. "Do *you* think Alex did it?"

"I don't know enough about it to have an opinion, Mike," Riel said. "But I'm sure Dave will sort it out."

For the next few minutes, neither of us spoke. I kept thinking about what Alex had said. I had a picture of it in my mind

"Alex said that when he found Sal, Sal was trying to say something." That was bothering me. "What do you think it was?"

Riel didn't answer, I guess because there was no way he could. But I couldn't stop thinking about it.

» » »

There was a buzz in the hallways at school the next day. Everyone was talking about Alex. Teddy was at his locker when I got to mine. We looked at each other, but neither of us said anything. When I went to the cafeteria at lunchtime, I noticed that Bailey wasn't at Teddy's table the way he usually was. I thought maybe he had stayed home from school, but, no, I spotted him outside. He was sitting on the bleachers. Annie was with him. I hesitated. I told myself that I should leave him alone, that it didn't make any difference anymore. But I couldn't make myself stay away.

Annie spotted me first. She touched Bailey's arm, and he glanced at me. He didn't move, not even when I climbed up to two rows below him. He looked tired. I wondered how long the police had kept him. I wondered if they had charged him with anything. I sure hoped so. After all, he had seen Alex in the alley with Sal. He had seen the blood on his clothes. He had told Alex to get out of there and to get rid of the clothes he'd been wearing. Even if he hadn't told the police that, I had. I bet Staci had, too. Or maybe he had made some kind of deal. He must have been the one who told the cops where Alex might have run to. How else did they know where to find him? And he had got Alex to come up out of the basement so that the cops didn't have to go down there to get him. Maybe Bailey had agreed to do those things in exchange for not being charged with anything.

I climbed up another row until I was standing right below him. He didn't look at me. Instead, he stood up and started to walk away. That did it. I climbed over the row that separated us and grabbed his arm. He tried to shake me off, but I held tight. He glowered at me.

"Alex said Sal was alive when you went into the alley,"

I said. "He was alive, and there were cops and an ambulance right down the street. But instead of calling them, you wasted your time telling Alex to get out of there."

Bailey tried again to jerk free of me.

"Maybe if you had called for help, he would still be alive," I said. "Did you ever think of that?"

Bailey's face was all red and twisted. I thought he was going to cry. Annie made her way over to where we were standing. She took his hand.

"He thinks about it all the time," she said quietly.

Bailey tried again to get free of me. This time I dropped my arm.

"Talk to him, Bailey," Annie said. "Maybe it'll help."

Bailey stared down at his feet. He was so still that it looked like he wasn't even breathing. Finally he said, "I wish I'd never even looked in that direction." Annie squeezed his hand. "But I did. He was walking away with Staci . . ." He was talking about Sal now. "And there was this big bang, and everybody turned to see what had happened. But I looked the other way. I saw Alex run out of school. He looked mad, and he was staring right at Sal. Sal must have seen him coming, because he ducked into the alley. Alex ran across the street. When I saw him go into the alley, I thought— " He let out a long, shaky sigh.

"You thought what?" I said.

"Tell him," Annie said gently. "Tell him what you told the police."

What was she talking about?

Bailey kept looking at his feet.

"The week before it happened, Bailey saw Alex try to hurt Sal," Annie said.

"*What?* What do you mean?" I looked at Bailey.

Bailey raised his head.

"I was on my way to my locker, and I saw Sal and Staci come out of a classroom together," he said. "It was late. I had to stay behind because I messed up another math quiz and Mr. Tran wouldn't leave me alone about it. He said if I didn't get extra help, I was only going to get further and further behind. Anyway, I saw Sal and Staci. They were talking and laughing. They looked like they were having a good time. They were walking toward the stairs. Then I saw Alex. He was standing near the stairs, and he was watching them. He looked really upset. He has this thing for Staci. She tutors him. He talks about her all the time. It really bugged him, seeing her talking to Sal and the two of them laughing like that. Then they stopped walking and Staci kissed Sal on the cheek, you know, how girls do sometimes. It doesn't necessarily mean anything. Then she went down a different hall, and Sal started down the stairs. I knew Alex was upset, but I didn't think he would—" He broke off and shook his head.

"You didn't think he would what?" I said.

"Alex pushed Sal down the stairs," Annie said.

I stared at her.

"Alex acts like a little kid sometimes," Bailey said. "But he's strong. He can really hurt you if he wants to.

He pushed Sal down the stairs. Then he ran down the stairs after him. I was afraid he was going to hit Sal or something. So I went after him. Sal had fallen all the way down to the landing. I ran down to where he was, grabbed Alex, and told him to get out of there. I had to tell him a couple of times because he wasn't listening to me at first. He was looking at Sal."

I couldn't believe that something like that had happened and Sal had never even mentioned it to me.

"Then I helped Sal up," Bailey said. "He was really shook up. He couldn't believe that Alex had pushed him. He said he wasn't hurt, but I saw his hands were shaking. I asked him if he was going to report Alex. I knew if he did, Ms. Rather or Mr. Gianneris would tell my mom."

Sal could have been seriously hurt. And what if Bailey hadn't come along when he did? What might have happened?

"If my mom had found out what Alex did, it would have been the last straw," Bailey said. "Alex's mom was my dad's sister. My parents are divorced. When Alex's mom died, Alex was supposed to go and live with my dad. But my dad is working on this big project in Singapore. My mom agreed to let Alex live with us until my dad comes back. But Alex keeps messing up, and my mom told him she's losing her patience. I was scared that if she found out what Alex did, she'd tell him he couldn't live with us anymore, and then what would happen to him?"

"What did Sal say?" I said, even though I was sure I already knew the answer.

"I told him I would talk to Alex. I told him I'd make sure Alex never did anything like that again. And he said okay, he wouldn't say anything. But he was still shaking when he walked the rest of the way down the stairs. You should have seen how tightly he was holding the railing."

I bet. I remembered coming out of the school with Sal the day before he died. I remembered him stopping at the top of the steps. I remembered the look on his face as he stood there, looking out at the street. I had seen Alex out there. Sal must have been afraid that Alex would try to hurt him again. But had he really been so scared of Alex that he had started to carry a knife?

"So when I saw Alex run into the alley behind Sal, I was worried," Bailey said. "I mean, Sal had just been walking down the street with Staci. He had his arm around her. Alex must have seen that. He must have got mad again. So I ran into the alley after him and—" His head twitched back and forth, like he was seeing everything he was describing but he still couldn't believe it. "He was on his knees beside Sal. There was blood all over his clothes. So I told him to get out of there. He had a sweatshirt in his backpack, and I made him put it on. It covered most of the blood. Then I made him get out of there. And I got out of there, too. I'm sorry. I'm sorry."

My hands were curled into fists. I wanted to punch him. I wanted to do it over and over again. But was he any more to blame than I was? It came back at me again. It washed right over me and left me shivering—if I hadn't told Rebecca that I had forgotten her book at home, I would have been with Sal. We would have gone downtown so he could take his driver's license test. Everything would have been different.

Annie was still holding his hand.

"I was doing what everyone else was doing," she said in a quiet voice. "I was looking in the other direction to see what had happened. Then I noticed that Bailey wasn't there anymore. I turned around and saw him come out of the alley. His face was white. I knew right away something was wrong. Then that woman came screaming out of the alley. So I went to see what had happened. Bailey followed me. Then he went over to where the knife was lying and it looked like he was going to pick it up—"

"I didn't see it the first time I was in there," Bailey said. "I wasn't thinking. When I saw it, I wanted to get rid of it."

"I told him not to touch it," Annie said. "I told him the woman had probably seen it. And by then some other kids had come into the alley, so I covered it with my scarf, you know, so no one would do anything stupid. And I called 911. I forgot about that woman who had been running to where the cops were. I wasn't thinking straight because . . ." She glanced at Bailey. There were tears in her eyes now.

"It's okay," Bailey said, squeezing her hand. "You might as well tell him."

"I wasn't thinking straight because at first I thought Bailey had something to do with it. So I asked him, and he told me he didn't. And I believed him. I knew Teddy didn't like Sal, but Bailey . . ." Her voice trailed off again.

"I didn't have anything against him," Bailey said. "He was okay."

"He panicked when he saw Sal lying there, that's all. He said he was afraid if the cops found out he'd gone into the alley before that woman found Sal, they would think he did it, you know, because of what had just happened out on the street. That's why he didn't do anything when he came out of the alley the first time. So I didn't tell the police that I'd seen Bailey go in there. I didn't tell them I saw him reaching for the knife. I mean, I called 911 even though that woman went running down the street to the police. I wasn't thinking straight, so I could see that maybe Bailey wasn't thinking straight, either." Tears trickled down her cheeks. Bailey put his arm around her and held her tightly. "I knew something was wrong, though. I knew he was hiding something. But he wouldn't even talk to me about it."

"Is that why you were fighting at Teddy's party?" I said.

"I knew there was something he wasn't telling me," Annie said.

"I asked her to believe me, and at first she did," Bailey said. "Then she said she wasn't sure, and that really scared me. If she didn't believe me and if she went to the cops, then for sure they wouldn't believe me, either."

She squeezed his hand this time.

"I asked Alex if he'd got rid of the clothes," Bailey said. "But I couldn't stop thinking about that knife. I was afraid they'd want to fingerprint everyone in the school or something."

I didn't tell him what I knew about the knife.

"Then I started thinking maybe I should go to the cops. But he's my cousin and . . ."

"The accident Alex was in," Annie said softly. "Bailey was driving the tractor. He shouldn't have been, but he was."

There were tears in Bailey's eyes.

"Did you tell Alex to say it was some man who did it?" I said.

Bailey shook his head. "He tried to tell me there was some man in the alley, but . . ."

"But what?" I said.

"Alex is like a little kid sometimes. He gets into trouble and he tries to blame someone else."

"You didn't believe him?" I said.

"He hit a kid in Regina," Bailey said. "With a piece of pipe. The kid was lucky he didn't lose an eye. Alex said he didn't do it, even though someone besides the guy saw him. He said it must have been someone else."

Oh.

"There was blood all over him," Bailey said. He looked miserable. "He's not bad. He really isn't. If you'd known him before the accident . . ."

Annie slipped an arm around his waist.

"They let me talk to him last night after they arrested him," Bailey said. "I told him he should do the right thing. I told him he had no choice. He should tell them what happened between him and Sal. I told him he should tell them he did it and that he was sorry. I said it would be better for everyone if he did that."

We stood there in silence for a few moments. Then I turned and made my way down the bleachers and went back into the school. I don't remember anything about any of my classes the rest of that day. Now that I knew what had happened, I didn't feel the way I thought I would. I thought I'd be happy it was all over. I thought I'd be jumping up and down. But I wasn't happy. Not even close. I kept thinking how stupid it was—Sal killed over a misunderstanding, because Alex *thought* that Sal was interested in Staci. I thought, too, how it could have been different if I hadn't left him that note.

After school I walked around for a while. I ended up at Vin's house. Vin looked surprised when he opened the door. No wonder—I was crying.

CHAPTER FIFTEEN

"I heard they arrested someone," Vin said. His mother was in the kitchen when I got to the house. She had called hello to me, but Vin hurried me up the stairs before she could see my face. We went to his room. I was sitting on Vin's bed. He was sitting on a chair. "So that's good, right, Mike?"

"Yeah," I said. "It turns out it was this kid from my school. He pushed Sal down the stairs the week before. I think Sal was really afraid of him." But that still bothered me. I thought we had been close. Had I been wrong about that? "Sal never said a word to me about it. A guy pushed him down the stairs, and he never mentioned it."

"Well, you know Sal. He never complained."

"I know. But you'd think that if he was scared enough to start carrying a knife, he would say something to somebody about it."

"Sal was carrying a knife?" Vin said. He stared at me, astonished. I remembered that I had told him the cops had asked me if Sal had a weapon. But at the time, even I hadn't known what kind of weapon they were talking about.

I had promised Riel I wouldn't say anything about the knife. But that was before the cops had arrested Alex. I didn't see what difference it would make now. It was case closed. So I told Vin about the knife that Annie had seen and that the cops were pretty sure that Sal had been stabbed to death with his own knife. I described it to him. He turned pale.

"What's the matter?" I said.

"It had a skull and crossbones and three sixes on it?" he said.

I nodded. "And an X."

He stood up slowly.

"What's the matter, Vin?"

"It's got to be a coincidence," Vin said.

"What's got to be a coincidence?"

"Did Annie say what the X looked like?"

"What do you mean, what it looked like? It looked like an X."

"Did she say if the X was painted on or scratched on, anything like that?"

"She said it looked like the X had been scratched into the handle. Why? Do you recognize the knife? Did you see him with it?"

He was shaking his head. "I'll be right back," he said.

He disappeared from the room. I heard him go down the stairs. A few minutes later, he came back and sat down on the chair again. His face was white. He stared at the floor for a few moments before looking up at me.

"What's going on, Vin?"

"Remember I said that my mom confiscated my knife?"

"Yeah."

"I just asked her. It wasn't her."

I got a weird, creepy feeling all over. "What are you talking about, Vin?"

"She says she didn't even know I had a knife. She's pretty steamed about it now that she knows. But she didn't take it."

Vin's knife was gone, and his mother hadn't taken it. My eyes met Vin's.

"Are you saying that *Sal* took your knife?"

"Either that or it's a huge coincidence. That knife Annie saw sounds just like mine. I scratched that X on the handle myself. I'd be able to tell if it was mine for sure it I saw it."

Now I was shaking my head.

"Sal knew I had it, Mike. I was fooling around with it that first time he came over. We were up here talking, and I was fooling around with it. Then my mom knocked on the door. She'd made us something to eat and was bringing it up. I put the knife in one of my drawers. I knew if my mom saw it, she'd go ballistic. A week or so later, I noticed it was gone. I figured she must have found it when she was cleaning my room. Man, I spent the next couple of days waiting for the roof to cave in. I thought she was going to ream me out for sure. But she didn't say a word. It turns out she didn't say anything because she *didn't* find it. She didn't know until two minutes ago that I even had it. Sal must have taken it." For a moment I thought he was going to cry. "Jeez, Mike, Sal was killed with *my* knife. If only I never had it. If only . . ."

I knew exactly how he felt.

We both just sat there, staring into space and thinking what we could have done differently.

Finally, I said, "I sure wish I'd known how scared he was of Alex."

"Yeah. If that kid was giving him a hard time for that long, you'd think he would have said something. Maybe he didn't think it would do any good. He said something about restraining orders when he was here."

"Restraining orders?"

"Yeah. That time he was over here. He was telling me this story about something he read in the paper. Something about a woman whose husband used to beat her up all the time. She got a restraining order, but it didn't do any good. Apparently the guy still went after her and killed her. Sal was all worked up about it, you know, about how sometimes there was nothing the cops could do until it was too late."

"When was this?" I said.

"That time he came over here. A few months ago. In the summer. I wish he would have said something."

So did I.

"You think I should tell the cops it was my knife?" Vin said.

"I don't know."

Vin was silent for another few moments. Then he

said, "Maybe you could talk to Riel about it, see what he says. It's okay with me. Whatever's right."

I told him I would do that.

>> >> >>

I was up in my room later, waiting for Riel to come home. The minute I heard him come through the door, I went downstairs. I waited until he had kissed Susan hello, and then I followed him through to the kitchen. He got himself something to eat and sat down at the table. I sat across from him and told him what Bailey had said. He listened carefully.

"So it looks like Alex really did it," I said. "I worked with him. I helped him. And he lied to me."

Then, because it seemed like the right thing to do, I told Riel what I had found out from Vin.

He didn't say what I thought he would. He didn't yell at me for talking about the knife with Vin. He didn't say that maybe if Vin hadn't had a knife, it never would have happened. Instead, he said, "I'll tell Dave what you told me." Then he said, "Tell Vin he did the right thing by speaking up, though."

I said I would.

It wasn't until I was in bed that it hit me.

I went downstairs again.

Riel was watching the news. Susan was curled up on the couch beside him. Her head was resting on his shoulder.

"I have to make a phone call," I said.

"It's pretty late, Mike."

"I have to call Vin. It's important."

I could tell he wasn't happy about that. Maybe he was worried that I was going to start hanging out with Vin again. But he didn't try to stop me.

I went into the kitchen, made the call, and apologized to Vin's mom when she answered.

"It's okay, Mike," she said. "I'm still up. Hang on. I'll get him for you."

"What's up?" Vin said a few moments later.

"When was the last time Sal was at your house?" I said.

"I told you. A few months ago. In the summer."

"When, exactly?"

"I don't know. I think it was the beginning of July. Yeah. It was right after the long weekend. I remember because my mom made these stupid cupcakes with red maple leafs on them. That's what she brought up for us when Sal was here."

"Did you see him after that?"

"Yeah, sure," Vin said. "A couple of times."

"Did he come to your house?"

"No. One time I went over to the McDonald's where he works. And one time he came over to my school and we went to that place I took you to—that restaurant near the library. I introduced him to Linzey."

"But he didn't go to your house again?"

"No. Why?"

"You're sure?"

"Yeah, I'm sure. What's up, Mike?"

"I'll tell you when I figure it out," I said.

I went back into the living room. I guess Riel read the expression on my face.

"Problem?" he said.

"If that knife really is Vin's, then I don't think Sal took it because he was afraid of Alex," I said. "He couldn't have. He didn't know Alex yet. Alex didn't move here until a couple of days before school started. Vin's knife went missing a few months ago, at the beginning of July."

Riel frowned. "He must have had some reason for taking it," he said.

"But what reason? Sal isn't one of those guys who carries a knife around to look tough." The kind of guy Vin used to be.

"Mike is right. He was such a sweet kid," Susan said. "Maybe he took it to make sure Vin didn't get into trouble."

"Maybe . . ." I said. Alex had told me he'd seen someone running out of the alley when he found Sal. What if he hadn't been lying to Bailey? I thought. What if he had been telling the truth? What if someone *else* had stabbed Sal? What if it was *that* person Sal was afraid of? What if he had taken Vin's knife because of that person? But *what* person? And why would Sal have been so scared that he thought he needed a knife? It didn't make sense.

CHAPTER SIXTEEN

I woke up feeling like I'd hadn't slept all night, which was more or less true. I'd tossed and turned, and I swear I saw every hour click by on the clock on my bedside table.

Sal had taken Vin's knife. He hadn't told anyone. What if he really had taken it to protect himself? Wouldn't he have said something to someone? I mean, if you're that scared, would you really keep it to yourself? And I was his friend. We had known each other for years. Why hadn't he talked to me?

I was on my way to school when it finally occurred to me that just because he hadn't told me, that didn't mean he hadn't told anyone. There was someone else Sal used to tell things to—things that he didn't tell me.

I had a spare right before lunch. I headed up to the park on the other side of the railroad tracks. There were two high schools up there, one on the east side of the park and one on the west side. I went to the one at the west side, and I waited. When the lunch bell rang, kids started to pour out of the place. There were three different exits that emptied onto the street, and I kept scanning all of them. But there was no guarantee she was even going to come out of school. Maybe she was going to meet up with her friends in the cafeteria.

Then I spotted her.

Imogen.

She had transferred schools at the end of the school year. Rebecca had told me it was because Sal broke up with her. She said Imogen really liked Sal and she didn't think she could stand being in the same school as him if she couldn't go out with him. Rebecca said that Imogen told her that the worst thing would be if Sal started going out with someone else and Imogen had to see them together in class or in the hall or in the cafeteria. I knew what she meant. I didn't think I'd be able to stand seeing Rebecca with another guy.

Imogen was with two other girls. She stopped walking when she saw me. For a moment I thought she was going to turn around and march right back into school so she wouldn't have to look at my face. But she didn't. She pulled herself up straight, like she was trying to show me she wasn't afraid, and she walked right up to me.

"What do you want, Mike?" she said.

"I need to talk to you. About Sal."

As soon as I said his name, her expression changed from snotty to sad.

"I heard they arrested the guy who did it," she said.

"Did you see Sal in July, Imogen?"

"Yeah. I went to that big picnic on the July first weekend," she said. "You know, the one that radio station puts on."

I knew it. It attracted mobs of people.

"I ran into Sal there and—" She shrugged. "When I saw him, I was ready to turn and run in the other direction. He was so mad at me when he found out what I did to you." She meant when he found out she had called the cops on me about that convenience store robbery. "But he said hi and we started talking and . . . it was like we never broke up."

Sal had gone over to Vin's house right after that weekend. Then Vin's knife had disappeared.

"Did he say if anything was bothering him?"

"What do you mean?"

"I don't know," I said. But I wished I did. "Did he say if anyone was bullying him or giving him a hard time, anything like that?"

"No."

"He didn't say if he was having problems with anyone?"

She shook her head, and I got discouraged. He hadn't said anything to Imogen, either, which made me think that there was nothing to say.

"Why?" Imogen said. "What's wrong?"

"Nothing, I guess."

Bailey must be right. Alex had done it, and then he'd lied about seeing a man run out of the alley. As for the knife, it was a complete mystery what Sal had been doing with it.

"What's going on, Mike?" Imogen said. "Why are you asking me all these questions?"

"I . . ." I looked at her. Was I going to sound crazy to

her? "I was just wondering if there was any reason Sal felt like he had to protect himself or anything like that, if something happened to him that weekend."

"We had a good time at the picnic," Imogen said. "Then he called me up the next day and asked me if I wanted to see a movie . . ." She frowned.

"What?" I said.

She shook her head.

"What, Imogen?"

"It's probably nothing," she said.

"What's probably nothing?"

"We went to see a movie down at the Paramount," she said. "After the movie was over, we got on the escalator. I was talking to him, and all of a sudden Sal got this look on his face."

"Look? What look?"

"Like he'd seen a ghost or something."

I remembered how he had looked when we came out of school together the day before he died.

"And?"

"And I asked him what was the matter. He was looking down at the bottom of the escalator. There were lots of people down there because we had gone to the early show. So there were all these people buying tickets for the next show. And there was this guy down there—just standing there. He really stuck out because everyone else was moving around. But he just seemed to be looking at Sal."

"What do you mean, seemed to be?"

"Well, that's what I thought at first. But when I turned my head to ask Sal if he knew that man, he didn't look scared anymore. I looked at the bottom of the escalator again, and the guy who had been looking at him—if that's what he was really doing—was gone. And Sal kind of laughed. He said he must have been seeing things."

"Did you ask him about the guy?"

"Well, no, because he put his arm around me and . . ." She frowned again. "But I remember thinking that we got out of there pretty fast after that and that Sal seemed in a big hurry to get to the subway. Why? What does that have to do with what happened to Sal? I heard they arrested a kid from your school."

"Do you remember what this guy looked like, Imogen?"

"It was months ago, Mike. And I just glanced at him."

"Do you remember anything at all?"

She thought for a minute. "Just that he had black hair. He seemed tall, but we were pretty far away. I mean, we were at the top of the escalator and he was at the bottom."

I told myself that a lot of people have dark hair. A whole lot of people.

"Thanks, Imogen," I said. I turned to go.

"Mike?"

"Yeah?"

"Sal said he wanted to tell you that we were back together. He said it didn't feel right keeping something like that from his best friend. But he knew how you felt about me, and he was afraid you'd get mad if he told you."

Imogen was pretty, but, if you ask me, she was nowhere near as pretty as Rebecca. She talked about people a lot more than Rebecca did, too, and from what I'd been able to tell, she liked to repeat things about people that weren't very nice. But I guess she must have had some good qualities, too. Otherwise, why would Sal have gotten back together with her? This was the first time that I had talked to her without thinking she was snotty and stuck-up. And that made me feel even worse about what had happened.

>> >> >>

I hurried back to school. It was still lunchtime, and because it was a nice day, there were a lot of kids outside. I scanned the sidewalk on both sides of the street until I found Teddy and his friends.

"Hey, Mike," Teddy said when I approached him. "I heard what happened. I heard it was Alex."

"Yeah," I said. "Teddy, you know the day Sal died—did you notice a man who might have been watching Sal? A tall man with black hair?" I tried to remember what else Alex had told me. "He might have been wearing a dark jacket."

Teddy shook his head. "Pretty much the only thing I was paying attention to that day was Staci."

I looked at the rest of his friends—Matt and Steven,

Sarah B.—everyone. I asked them all the same question.

Sara D. was the one who surprised me. "I remember seeing a guy like that," she said.

"You do?"

"Black hair. Tall guy. Dark jacket. It had a red stripe across it." That was exactly what Alex had said. "He was staring at me. I thought he was kind of creepy."

"You're sure?" I said. "You saw this guy?"

"Like I said," she said.

"Where did you see him?"

"The first time, he was over there, in front of the travel agency."

The travel agency was a couple of stores away, past the entrance to the alley. What if it was the same guy Imogen had seen at the movie theater? And what if Sal had been afraid of him for some reason? What if he'd seen that guy that day? What if he had ducked into the alley to avoid him?

"Did you see the guy go into the alley?"

"No," she said.

Wait a minute. What had she just said?

"What do you mean, Sara, *the first time?* Did you see him *again* after that?"

"Like I said, the first time I saw him, I thought he was some kind of creep. The way he was staring, he looked like he could be a serial killer or something. Then, when I saw him again and found out who he was, I figured he was hanging around because he wanted to talk to kids."

"What do you mean? You know who he is?"

"Sure," she said. "He's a reporter." She was looking at me funny now. "It was that guy who crashed into you that day when you were coming out of school carrying a box. You and that guy collided. I was outside, remember?"

I did. She had laughed at me.

"The guy said he was a reporter, remember?"

"*That's* the guy you saw staring at you that day?"

"Yeah," she said. "Why?"

"Would you tell the police that if they asked you?"

"What's going on, Mike?" Teddy said.

"I'm not sure. But it could be important. Would you tell them, Sara?"

"Yeah, she will," Teddy said. Sara didn't argue with him.

» » »

I knew I should have found a phone and called Riel right away. But the community newspaper office was right down the street, and something pulled me toward it. I wanted to see the guy. I wanted to make sure he was still there.

The newspaper office was mostly one big room filled with desks and computers. There was a long counter just inside the door. A woman was sitting behind it. She looked up at me.

"Can I help you?" she said.

I was already scanning the room, but I didn't see him.

"Gil Anderson," I said. "Is he here?"

She glanced over her shoulder.

"Hey, Gil," she called. "Someone here to see you."

I scanned the room again. I still didn't see him.

A short, balding man came up to the counter and looked expectantly at me. "I'm Gil Anderson," he said. "You wanted to see me?"

» » »

I went straight to the school office and called Riel from the phone that students can use when they need to call home. I told him I had something important to talk to him about. I said it had to do with Sal. He said he'd pick me up right after school, and sure enough, his car was waiting outside when the final bell rang. I got in and told him everything that Imogen and Sara D. had said. I reminded him what Alex had said he saw when he went into the alley. Then I told him about my visit to the newspaper office.

"You say this guy gave you his business card?" Riel said. I nodded. "Where is it?"

"At home."

Riel drove us home, and I ran up to my room to look for the card. It was in the box of stuff that I had brought home from Sal's locker, right under the love letter in the pink envelope from Imogen. I took it down to Riel and he examined it.

"I went there," I told him. "I talked to Gil Anderson. It wasn't the same guy."

"What's this phone number?" Riel said, turning the card over.

"The guy I talked to said it was his cell phone number."
Riel called the number. He listened, frowning, and
hung up. "I just got a generic voice mail message. No
name." He made another call, this one to Dave Jones.
When he finished that call, he said, "Dave wants to talk
to you in person. Come on."

Half an hour later I was explaining it all to Dave.

"Sal was afraid of something back in July," I said.
"He took Vin's knife right after that. Imogen saw a man
who matched the description of the man Sara D. said she
saw hanging around the school that day. Sara described
the guy to me. It sounds like the same guy Alex saw. He
was wearing the same jacket. And I bumped right into
him a few days after Sal was killed. I got a good look at
him. So did Sara."

I was afraid Dave wouldn't take me seriously, but
then Riel added, "This guy was asking Mike a lot of
questions. And he went to the school and tried to get
more information about Mike."

"Exactly what did he say when he spoke to you,
Mike?"

"Just that he was writing an article on youth violence
and that he wanted to interview me. He said he saw me
on the news."

"Okay," Dave said. "You sit tight. I'll get someone to
go the newspaper office and speak to Gil Anderson. In
the meantime, let's see if we can put together a composite of this guy and figure out who he is."

I hesitated. "So you believe me?" I said.

"I believe you saw the guy. And I want to talk to Sara again. And to Imogen."

I spent a long time looking at pictures on a computer to see if the man I had seen had a police record. If he did, I didn't see him. So then I had to try to come up with a description for a computerized picture of what he looked like. I'm not that good at describing people—usually I don't pay that much attention to whether someone has a long nose or a thin nose, how close together their eyes are, how thick their eyebrows are, that kind of thing. So mostly I was thinking, *no, that's not right*, and *that's not right, either.* Nobody was more surprised than me when I finally found myself staring at a pretty good likeness of the guy. By the time I had finished, Dave had found out that although the business card belonged to Gil Anderson, who really was the man I had met in the newspaper office, the cell phone number on the back wasn't his. Gil Anderson said that he gave out a lot of business cards. He said he couldn't begin to guess how many people had one. Dave said he was going to show the composite to Imogen and Sara D. to see if we were all talking about the same person. Then he thanked me for coming in, and Riel and I left.

"Now what?" I said.

"Now we wait," Riel said.

CHAPTER SEVENTEEN

"Are you okay, Mike?" Riel said. We were sitting at the kitchen table, eating supper. Susan wasn't home. It turned out that as an emergency room doctor, her shifts were even crazier than Riel's. Some weeks it seemed like she didn't even live with us, because she'd be sleeping when I left for school and she'd be at work when I got home, and she wouldn't get out of the hospital again until after I was in bed.

"I was just thinking," I said.

"About Sal?"

"About the guy Alex said he saw in the alley. I don't get it. Why would he want to hurt Sal? Why was Sal so afraid of him?"

"You're assuming he was," Riel said.

"Imogen said Sal looked scared that time she saw the guy. And you should have seen the look on his face when we came out of school the day before he died. He was definitely scared of something. I thought it was Alex. But what if he saw that guy out there on the street and I just didn't notice? There were a lot of people out on the street. There always are at lunchtime."

"I hope you're not blaming yourself, Mike," Riel said.

Boy, if he only knew.

"If Sal saw this guy in July—"

"Assuming it's the same man," Riel said.

"If he saw him in July, and he saw him again the day before he died, and if he was afraid of him, then that means he must have known the guy, right?" I said. "Otherwise why would he be afraid of him? But how would Sal get to know someone who scared him so much?"

"Sal dealt with the public a lot in his job," Riel said. "Maybe it has to do with something that happened at work."

"But then why didn't someone at work say something to the police? I mean, if someone he worked with saw him in a fight or something like that . . . " Then I remembered what Tulla had told me. "There's been a lot of turnover at the restaurant," I said. "And if Sal was scared of that guy in July, then whatever happened to scare him must have happened before that." I remembered that Dave had come to our school and that the police had put out an appeal to parents of kids who went to our school and to the other schools in the area, kids who hung around down on Gerrard Street at lunchtime. The police had done exactly what I had done. They had focused on kids who went to school near where it had happened.

"I'm sure Dave is taking all the right steps, Mike," Riel said.

I was sure he was, too. But that didn't stop a whole bunch of questions from eating at me.

"Why didn't Sal say something?" I said. *Especially to me*, I thought. I was his best friend. Well, I was supposed to have been his best friend. But I had let him down. "You know what Sal was like. If he was so scared, why didn't he go to the police? Why did he steal Vin's knife instead?"

All Riel could do was shake his head. He didn't have any more answers than I did.

» » »

I'm not stupid. At least, I'm not stupid when it comes to cops. I know that things take a lot longer in real life than they do on TV. So I didn't really expect anything to have changed between the time I went to bed Thursday night and the time I got up again on Friday morning. But that didn't stop me from hoping. I went downstairs to see if Riel was still home and whether he had had any news. But he wasn't there. Susan was. She was sitting at the kitchen table, drinking coffee and reading the newspaper. She looked nice and relaxed, and she smiled at me.

"Good morning, Mike. Can I get you something?"

"No, I'm good," I said. Riel was very big on my looking after myself and not expecting Susan to do everything just because now she was married to him. I got myself some cereal and juice and sat down at the table with her.

"Did you see John this morning?" I said.

Susan gave me a funny look. Her smile got even

brighter. Duh! Of course she'd seen him. I could feel myself turning red in the face.

"What I mean is, did he say anything—about Sal, I mean?"

"He told me what you told Dave," she said. "But that's all."

I tried not to feel disappointed. It was too soon for anything to have happened. But just because you know something probably hasn't happened yet, that doesn't stop you from wishing that it had.

» » »

I went to school. Then I went home and got ready to go to work. Riel pulled up just as I was leaving the house.

"I'll give you a lift," he said. I got into the car. "You know that guy you saw?" he said. "It looks like maybe you were onto something."

"Really?"

"Dave tracked down some of Sal's former coworkers, people who worked at the restaurant before the summer. Somebody recognized the guy. They'd seen him in the place a few times. They think he's the boyfriend of someone who used to work there."

"So they know who he is?"

"They have a first name. They're trying to track him down. They definitely want to talk to him. It's a good lead, Mike." The way he said it, it sounded like he was proud of me. I kind of wished he wasn't.

When he dropped me at work, he said, "Susan's going to a baby shower tonight, so she probably won't be home when you get home. And I'm probably going to be out, too. I thought I'd go watch a game with some of the guys."

Cop guys, he meant. Mostly Riel was home in the evenings. But sometimes, especially if Susan was busy or working, he hung out with guys from work. Well, why not?

» » »

It was quiet at work. Alex wasn't there, which meant that nothing got dropped and there was no one for Mr. Geordi to yell at. You would have thought that would put a smile on his face, but it didn't. He grumbled at everyone. One time he stood behind me while I was putting canned fish on the shelf, and when I was finished, he turned a couple of the cans a few millimeters so that they were exactly straight on the shelf, and then he scowled at me as if to tell me, How come you couldn't do it right? But it didn't matter to me. I had other things to think about.

The house was dark when I got home, and neither Susan's car nor Riel's car was in the driveway. I unlocked the front door and pushed it open. I was in the front hall, wondering if there was anything good to eat in the fridge, when I saw a light at the top of the stairs. I was glad that I'd gotten home first. Riel was fanatical about turning off the lights whenever you left a room. I forgot a lot, which meant that I got called back to whatever room it was where I'd left a light on. Riel never shut off the light for me. He always said that if he made me come back and do it myself, maybe I would remember the next time. But I'd forgotten again.

I shut the door and locked it. Riel insisted on that, too. When I first moved in, I used to be as bad with the lock as I was with the lights. That's because when I lived with my uncle Billy, he always used to tell me not to lock the door when I went to bed. Billy partied a lot, which meant he came home drunk a lot, and he hated to fumble around for his keys.

As soon as I shut the door, the light at the top of the stairs went off. Maybe it had burned out. I decided to take a look, but before I even put my foot on the bottom step, someone came hurtling down the stairs.

"Hey!" I shouted.

At first I thought he was going to run right out of the house. But he didn't. Instead, he grabbed me. He was tall and strong. He was wearing gloves and a balaclava, so I couldn't see his face, just angry-looking eyes and a twisted mouth.

"Where is she?" he said.

I struggled to get away from him, but his hands were biting into my arms. He shook me so hard my teeth rattled.

That's when I saw that he had something else in his hands besides my arms. It was an envelope. A pink envelope. The love letter from Imogen that had been in Sal's locker. What did he want that for?

"Where is she?" he said again.

"I don't know what you're talking about," I said.

He pushed me backward across the front hall and slammed me up against the wall.

"You said you were his best friend. He must have said something to you. Where is she?"

When I didn't answer, he slammed me into the wall again. It felt like all the air had been knocked out of my lungs.

"Where is she?"

I wanted to shout for help, but I couldn't catch my breath. He slammed me into the wall a third time, harder this time, so hard that I felt like I had fallen ten stories onto a concrete floor. His hands were like vices. I tried to work myself free, but his grip only got tighter. I looked into his eyes. That's when I knew, I just knew, that he was going to kill me. I could see it in his eyes. They were brown—I know they were—but there was a cold blackness in them. He pulled me off the wall again. He was going to slam me back against it. He was going to do it over and over again. He was going to kill me.

After that, everything slowed down. I felt myself being pulled forward. I looked into those cold, dead eyes. I remembered the look on Sal's face the day before he died. I saw the man holding me now. I felt his arms start to move again as he got ready to slam me backward. I couldn't move my arms. I couldn't resist.

So I kneed him.

I kneed him as hard as I could in the most vulnerable place I could.

He grunted. His knees buckled. But he didn't let go of me. If anything, his hands bit more deeply into my arms. I kneed him again, as hard as I could.

He let out a roar. His grip slipped for a split second, and I got one arm free. I reached out and grabbed the balaclava off his head.

It was him.

It was the same guy I had seen outside my school, the one who had told me he was a reporter.

I tried to get my other arm free, but before I could he had me pinned against the wall again.

I decided to kick him and to keep on kicking him as many times as it took. But he slammed me into the wall so hard this time that pain exploded in my back and I couldn't breathe. I would have slid to the floor if he hadn't been holding onto me. He had been mad enough before. Now he was enraged.

Maybe that was why he didn't hear the little scrabbly sound of a key going into a lock. Maybe it was why he didn't hear the key turn.

Please don't let it be Susan, I thought. *Please.*

I wanted to shout out a warning. But I was gasping for breath, and he was getting ready to hammer me for a fifth time.

Riel stepped into the front hall.

He looked at me.

He looked at the man.

He started toward him.

But by then the guy had seen Riel. He let go of me

and ran through the living room and into the kitchen. He was heading for the back door.

Riel gave me an once-over. "Are you okay?" he said.

I nodded.

"Call 911," Riel said. He sprinted out the front door to try to intercept the guy.

I slumped to the floor and sat there for a moment, trying to catch my breath. When I tried to get to my feet, my knees buckled. I crawled to the phone, reached up for it, and called 911 like Riel had said. I told the dispatcher what had happened. I also told her that it was Riel's house and that he was a police officer and that he was chasing the guy.

Riel was back a couple of minutes later.

"I lost him," he said, panting. He sounded disgusted with himself. "Are you okay, Mike?"

"My back," I said. Riel reached down to help me up. I winced when he pulled my arm. Riel frowned. When he got me to my feet, he turned me around and lifted my T-shirt to take a look. I told him what had happened. "I thought he was going to kill me," I said.

Riel looked at me for a long time. Then he said, "Come and sit down. As soon as the police get here, I'll take you to the ER and have you checked out."

When we got into the living room, I saw a pink envelope lying on the floor.

"He had that in his hand," I said. "It's from Sal's locker." I explained to Riel what I was doing with it. "I was bringing the box home when that guy bumped into me at school. A bunch of stuff fell out, and he helped me pick it up." I thought back to exactly what had happened. "He was looking at that envelope like he was dying to see what was in it. I thought he was just some nosy reporter. I thought it was a love letter to Sal from Imogen. But if that's all it was, why did he have it in his hands when he attacked me?"

Riel opened the envelope and pulled out a single sheet of pink paper. He scanned it.

"It's not from Imogen," he said. "It's from someone named Carole." He looked at the envelope again. "There's no return address. None inside, either. This Carole, she's thanking Sal for everything he did."

"What did he do?"

"She doesn't say. All she says is that she's safe and that he shouldn't worry about her and that she'll keep in touch. That's it."

I wondered who this Carole was and why the guy had wanted that letter so badly.

» » »

The police came. Riel talked to them and told them that Homicide was looking for the guy who had attacked me. He called Dave and spoke to him while one of the cops took a statement from me. Then Riel locked up the house and took me to the hospital to have me checked out. It turned out I didn't have any broken bones, but the doctor who looked at me said he would be surprised if

220

my whole back didn't turn black and blue. I had to sleep on my stomach that night. Even so, my back felt like it was on fire. Susan gave me some extra-strength pain reliever when we got home. She said it would also help me sleep, but she was wrong. I woke up two or three times, each time because I'd had a nightmare. Each time it was the same nightmare. The guy was slamming me against the wall again and again and again, but in my dream, Riel didn't show up to stop him. In my dream, I was on my own.

CHAPTER EIGHTEEN

Riel knocked on my door the next morning. I couldn't believe how much it hurt when I tried to sit up. My back felt like a five-hundred-pound gorilla had been using it as a trampoline—which, I guess, was pretty close to what had happened.

"You asked me to make sure you got up on time," Riel said. "You said you wanted to meet Rebecca's bus. How about I run you down there?"

I said okay. Then I said, "Did they find the guy yet?"

"Not yet. But they're looking, Mike. They've got his full name now, they know where he lives, and they've got some pictures from his place. They're checking that letter for fingerprints, too. They'll get him."

"Do they know why he did it?"

"Not yet. It's a safe bet it has something to do with this Carole, though. Apparently she was his girlfriend—and she used to work at the same McDonald's as Sal. One of his neighbors says he suspects Hanson—that's his name, Daniel Hanson—was physically abusive to this Carole."

I remembered what the letter had said.

"Do you think Sal helped her? Do you think that's

why she wrote him?"

"Maybe. They found Sal's laptop at Hanson's place."

"So he's the one who broke into Sal's place?"

"It looks like it," Riel said. "Maybe he was looking for some information about Carole. Hurry up and get dressed, Mike. You don't want to disappoint Rebecca."

» » »

I was waiting in the school parking lot when the bus pulled in. Rebecca ran to me as soon as she got off. She threw her arms around me and hugged me so tightly that I thought I would faint from the pain. I didn't mean to, but I groaned. She pulled back a little so that she could look at me.

"What's wrong?" she said.

"It's a long story," I said.

When I finally told her—after she had loaded her suitcase into her parents' car and told her mother she would be home in a little while, and after we had gone into a coffee place near school and ordered something to drink—she held both my hands and said in a small voice, "He could have killed you, Mike." A tear ran down her cheeks. I squeezed her hands and told her I was fine.

"What did you want to tell me, Rebecca?"

She looked puzzled.

"The last time I talked to you on the phone, it sounded like you wanted to tell me something important. What was it?"

"It's nothing," she said. She held my hand all the way home, too, and didn't seem to mind that we had to walk slower than usual.

» » »

Riel let me stay home from school on Monday. He told me to keep all the doors locked. He said if I heard anything, anything at all, or if I was scared about anything, anything at all, I should call him right away.

"I mean it, Mike," he said.

I said okay.

Around two o'clock I heard something.

I tensed up.

I'd been lying on my bed, but now I slid off it. I tiptoed across my room and got my baseball bat out of the closet. I had it in my hand as I crept down the hall toward Riel's room for the phone. Then someone called out my name.

It was Riel.

He came upstairs. He looked serious, as usual, but I could see that he wanted to tell me something.

"They arrested Daniel Hanson in the airport in Calgary about twenty minutes ago," he said.

"*Calgary?*" I said.

"The postmark on that envelope was Calgary. If he was looking for Carole, it was a good bet he'd head out there. The Calgary police have him."

"Did he confess to killing Sal?"

"No," Riel said. "But when they did a thorough search of his place, they found traces of blood. If he stabbed Sal, there's a good chance he got some blood on himself. They didn't find any clothes with blood on them. But there was some blood between the floorboards just inside his back door. According to Dave, it looks like a transfer from the bottom of a shoe. He may have washed the floor, but some of the blood got into the cracks. There's enough to test for DNA. In the meantime, they're holding him for break and enter both here and at Sal's parents' place, for theft, and for aggravated assault on you. They could bump that up to attempted murder." I started to shake when he said that. "And now that he's in custody, they've put an appeal out to this Carole. They're asking her to come forward. She may be able to shed some light on this."

"What about Alex?"

"They let him go."

Poor Alex. I felt sorry for him. Getting arrested must have been scary enough. But it had to have been much, much worse that both Bailey and his mother thought that Alex had done it. They'd actually thought he'd killed someone.

» » »

I had the next weekend off for a change, and I was glad because, finally, it was all over. It turned out the blood they found in Daniel Hanson's house was Sal's blood.

And Hanson's ex-girlfriend Carole came forward. She was living in a small town in British Columbia. She didn't even know Sal had been killed until she saw an article in the newspaper saying that the police were looking for her and wanted to ask her some questions in relation to a murder investigation. She went to her local police station. Then Dave flew out west and talked to her in person. When he got back to town, he came to the house and filled us in. He told us that Carole had been shaking like a leaf the whole time. She said that at first everything had been fine between her and Hanson. He seemed like a nice, considerate guy. She said that he was a little on the jealous side but that she'd been flattered by his attention. Then he started getting possessive. He didn't want her to go anywhere without him. He hit her a few times. Once, she called the police, but he told her that even if they arrested him, they couldn't keep him for long, and when he got out, he would kill her. So when the police came, she told them that the only reason she called was that she was mad at him.

"The officers who took that call should have pressed it," Dave said. "They're supposed to with domestic cases."

After that, things got worse. She was scared of him. She confided in Sal. She said that she'd gotten to know Sal and that he was always nice, even though he was so young. Sal told her that she should go to the police. But she was too afraid. Then one day Hanson came to the McDonald's where they worked and saw her talking to Sal. He became even more jealous. He started pressuring her to quit her job. He beat her up. She came to work with bruises all over her. This time Sal finally convinced her. He called the police for her, and Hanson was arrested.

"He got six months," Dave said with disgust. "He was out in two."

But by then, Carole was gone. She'd packed up everything and moved out of town. Sal had helped her. She said maybe Hanson had gone after Sal because he thought Sal knew where she was. But he didn't. Carole wrote to him a couple of times, but she never gave a return address, and she always arranged to have the letter mailed from somewhere else.

When the police told Hanson that Carole had come forward, he went berserk, Dave said. Then they told him about the blood they had found at his house. They said they were going to charge him with first-degree murder on Sal and attempted murder on me. They said he was going to be in prison for life.

That's when his lawyer made a deal.

Hanson would plead guilty to second-degree murder on Sal and aggravated assault on me and, in return, would be eligible for parole in fifteen years.

"Fifteen years?" I said. "Is that all?"

"For second-degree murder, you get life in prison, same as first-degree murder. The only difference is that you're eligible for parole earlier," Riel said. "But being eligible for parole in fifteen years doesn't mean you automatically get out in fifteen years."

"Hanson's a dangerous guy," Dave said. "But if he wants to think he has a shot, he can be my guest."

Hanson told the cops that when he got out of jail after the assault on Carole and found that she had taken off, he started to look for her. He went to the restaurant and asked around. He talked to Sal. Sal denied that he knew where she was. But Hanson didn't believe him.

"He says he tried to scare Sal," Dave said. "He'd hang around the restaurant. One time Sal went up to him and told him if he didn't get lost, he'd call the police. Hanson seemed to think that was pretty funny. He asked what Sal was going to tell them—that there was a man standing on a public sidewalk outside of McDonald's?"

Hanson asked Sal a couple of times where Carole was, and Sal always said the same thing: he didn't know. Then Hanson started showing up places where Sal was—like the movie theater. And Sal got scared.

"Hanson saw him again the day after the movie theater. Sal told him if he saw him around again, he was going to call the police. And Hanson said the same thing—*and tell them what?* He told Sal that if he did call the police, even if the police did nothing—which he was pretty sure they would—Sal would be sorry. That must have been when Sal took your friend's knife. Right after that, Hanson disappeared."

"What do you mean, disappeared?" I said.

"He got into a fight—a case of road rage. He went to jail on that. He was locked up for three months over the summer. Got out at the end of September."

It started to make sense.

"Sal probably thought he'd given up," I said. "He took the knife from Vin at the beginning of the summer because he was scared. Then Hanson dropped out of sight. Maybe that's why he didn't say anything. Maybe he thought Hanson wasn't a threat after all—until he saw him out on the street the day before he died."

"Hanson says he saw that whole thing on the street with all those kids," Dave said. "He says that when Sal saw him, he ducked into that alley. Hanson thought that was funny. He said that Sal looked like he was going to—well, he looked scared. So Hanson followed him. The guy is 100 percent bully. He's probably a psychopath. Sal told him to stay away or else. He pulled out a knife. Hanson said, 'Or else what?' He's a big guy."

And strong. I knew that from personal experience.

"He said it was easy to turn that knife on Sal."

Jeez. Sal had been holding the knife, and Hanson had wrapped his hands around Sal's hands and killed him.

"I wish Sal had said something to me," I said. "I would have made sure he talked to the police."

Dave and Riel looked at each other. Then Riel said, gently, "If Hanson didn't actually threaten Sal, I'm not sure things would have turned out much differently, Mike," he said. "So don't blame yourself for what happened."

I felt terrible. I had to tell somebody. I decided it would be Rebecca. It didn't seem right that Teddy knew and she didn't.

I went over to Rebecca's house. She invited me in, but I said, no, I'd rather go for a walk or something. I didn't want to be in her house because I was pretty sure she'd ask me to leave as soon as I told her what I had to say.

"I lied to you," I said.

She just looked at me.

"The day Sal died, I said I left your textbook at home, but I didn't." Teddy had seen the book in my locker. Then he had read the note I left for Sal. He knew what I'd done. "I lied to you, Rebecca. And to Sal."

"I know," she said.

"What?"

"I know."

"But how—"

"When I went up to you on the street, you were coming from home. But you weren't carrying anything. You didn't have my book with you. The next morning, I was waiting for you at your locker when you got to school. I asked you for my book. You took it out of your locker and you gave it to me. I didn't think about it at the time. In fact, I didn't think about it until I was in Quebec City, doing homework. That's when it hit me— when could you possibly have put it in your locker? You couldn't have brought it from home that morning. If you had, you would have taken it out of your backpack, not your locker."

I was so ashamed of myself.

"I didn't forget it at home," I said finally.

"Then why did you tell me you did?" she said. She didn't sound mad, which confused me.

I didn't know what to say.

"Mike?" She took my hand and made me look at her.

"I . . ." I looked into her brown eyes. I wondered if I'd ever be able to do that again once I'd told her. "I wanted some excuse not to go downtown with Sal," I said. "I was mad at him."

She let go of my hand. Uh-oh.

"How come?" she said.

"Remember when you met us outside the day before he died? I asked him what he was going to say to me and he said it wasn't important, he would tell me later?"

She nodded.

"Well, he called me that night."

"And?"

"He told me he was going out with Imogen again. He said he'd been going out with her all summer. And I got mad at him. I thought he was my friend. He broke up with her after he found out what she'd done to me. And now he was back together with her, like it was all okay with him."

Rebecca just looked at me. I couldn't tell what she was thinking, and that scared me.

"I guess he loved her, Mike," she said finally. "And I know she's sorry for what she did. I guess he loved her enough to give her a second chance."

She was probably right.

Sal had forgiven Imogen. But would anyone forgive me for what I'd done? I'd bailed on Sal at the last minute, and that had changed everything. If I hadn't lied, if I hadn't left that note, we would have gone downtown together. Sal would have written the test for his driver's license. He wouldn't have been anywhere near that alley. He would still be alive. I had been living with that for weeks now, and I couldn't imagine anyone giving *me* a second chance.

I looked at Rebecca. Her face was so serious. She reached out and took my hand.

"It wasn't your fault, Mike," she said. She sounded so positive. I wished I could feel the same way, but I couldn't.

Rebecca pulled me to her and wrapped her arms around me. We stood there like that for a long time.

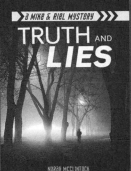